'Seasoned with sunshine, ... lightness of touch and humour is gi... ... y t... ...eeply unpleasant crimes and slippery characters ... The Inspector's cure for incipient melancholia is a plateful of caponata or grilled mullet, followed by a walk and a cigarette. Mine would be the next Montalbano novel'
Daily Express

'The novels of Andrea Camilleri breathe out the sense of place, the sense of humour, and the sense of despair that fill the air of Sicily. To read him is to be taken to that glorious, tortured island'
Donna Leon

'The seal of the best foreign crime writing is as much the stylish prose as the unfamiliar settings. When both ingredients are presented with the expertise shown by Andrea Camilleri, the result is immensely satisfying'
Independent

'For sunny views, explosive characters and a snappy plot constructed with great farcical ingenuity, the writer you want is Andrea Camilleri'
New York Times

'Among the most exquisitely crafted pieces of crime writing available today ... simply superb'
Sunday Times

THE DANCE OF THE SEAGULL

Andrea Camilleri is one of Italy's most famous contemporary writers. His books have sold over 65 million copies worldwide. He lives in Rome. The Inspector Montalbano series has been translated into thirty-two languages, was adapted for Italian television and screened on BBC4. *The Potter's Field*, the thirteenth book in the series, was awarded the Crime Writers' Association's International Dagger for the best crime novel translated into English.

Stephen Sartarelli is an award-winning translator. He is also the author of three books of poetry, most recently *The Open Vault*. He lives in France.

ANDREA CAMILLERI

THE DANCE OF THE SEAGULL

Translated by Stephen Sartarelli

PICADOR

First published 2013 by Penguin Books,
a member of Penguin Group (USA) Inc., New York

First published in Great Britain 2013 by Mantle

This paperback edition published in Great Britain 2013 by Picador
an imprint of Pan Macmillan Ltd
Pan Macmillan, 20 New Wharf Road, London N1 9RR
Basingstoke and Oxford
Associated companies throughout the world
www.panmacmillan.com

ISBN 978-1-4472-2872-1

Copyright © Sellerio Editore 2009
Translation copyright © Stephen Sartarelli 2013

Originally published in Italian 2009 as *La Danza de Gabbiano* by Sellerio Editore, Palermo

The right of Andrea Camilleri to be identified as the
author of this work has been asserted by him in accordance
with the Copyright, Designs and Patents Act 1988.

1 3 5 7 9 8 6 4 2

A CIP catalogue record for this book is available from the British Library.

Typeset by SetSystems Ltd, Cambridge, CB22 3GN
Printed and bound by CPI Group (UK) Ltd, Croydon, CR0 4YY

Visit **www.panmacmillan.com** to read more about all our books
and to buy them. You will also find features, author interviews and
news of any author events, and you can sign up for e-newsletters
so that you're always first to hear about our new releases.

THE DANCE OF THE SEAGULL

ONE

At about five thirty in the morning, he could no longer bear to lie in bed with his eyes wide open, staring at the ceiling.

This had started with the onset of old age. Normally, after midnight, he would lie down, read for half an hour, and as soon as his eyelids began to droop, he would close the book, turn off the lamp on the bedside table, get in the right position — which was always on his right side, knees bent, right hand open, palm up, on the pillow, cheek resting on his hand — close his eyes, and fall asleep immediately.

Often he was lucky enough to sleep through till morning, all in one stretch, but on other nights, such as the one that had just ended, he would wake up for no reason, after barely a couple of hours of sleep, unable for the life of him to fall asleep again.

Once, on the verge of despair, he'd got up and drunk half a bottle of whisky in the hope that it would put him to sleep. The result was that he'd turned up at the police station at dawn, completely drunk.

He got up and went to open the French windows leading onto the veranda.

The dawning day was a thing of beauty. All polished and clean, it looked like a just-painted picture, the paint still wet. The sea, however, was a little rougher than usual.

He went outside and shuddered from the cold. It was already mid-May. Normally it would be almost as hot as in the summer, whereas it still felt like March.

And it looked as if the day would go to the dogs by late morning. To the right, behind Monte Russello, a few black clouds were already gathering slowly.

He went inside, into the kitchen, and made coffee. Drinking the first cup, he went into the bathroom. He came out dressed, poured a second cup of coffee, and went out onto the veranda to drink it.

'Up bright an' early this mornin', Inspector!'

Montalbano raised a hand in greeting.

It was Mr Puccio, pushing his boat into the water. He climbed aboard and started to row, heading for the open sea.

For how many years had Montalbano watched him go through the same motions?

He lost himself gazing at a seagull in flight.

Nowadays one didn't see many seagulls. They'd moved into town. And there were hundreds even in Montelusa, a good six miles from the coast. It was as if they had grown tired of the sea and were staying away. Why were they reduced to foraging through urban refuse for food instead of feasting on the fresh fish in the sea? Why did they stoop to squabbling with rats over a rotten fish head? Had they abased themselves on purpose, or had something changed in the natural order?

Suddenly the gull folded its wings and dived towards the beach. What had it seen? But when its beak touched the sand, instead of rising back up in the air with its prey, it crumpled into a pile of feathers lightly fluttering in the early morning wind. Maybe it had been shot, though the inspector hadn't heard any gunshots. What kind of idiot would shoot a seagull, anyway? The bird, which lay about thirty paces from the veranda, was most certainly dead. But then, with Montalbano looking on, it sort of shuddered, pulled itself up, staggering to its feet, leaned entirely to one side, opened one wing, the one closer to the sand, and started spinning round, the tip of its wing inscribing a circle, its beak unnaturally pointed to the sky, its neck twisted out of shape. What was it doing? Dancing? Dancing and singing. Actually, no, it wasn't singing, the sound coming from its beak was hoarse, desperate, as if it was crying for help. And every so often, still turning round and round, it stretched its neck rather unnaturally upwards, waving its beak back and forth, like an arm and a hand trying to place something high up but not managing to reach it.

In a flash Montalbano jumped onto the beach and stopped a pace away from the bird. It showed no sign of having seen him, but immediately its spinning motion became more uncertain and unsteady, until finally, after making a very shrill noise that sounded human, it staggered, as the wing gave out from under it, and it collapsed to one side and died.

It danced to its own death, the inspector thought, shaken by what he'd just seen.

But he didn't want to leave the bird to the dogs, to the ants. Picking it up by the wings, he brought it to the veranda, then went into the kitchen to get a plastic bag. He put the bird in it and ballasted the package with two heavy stones he kept around the house as ornaments, then took off his shoes, trousers, and shirt, and went onto the beach in his underpants and into the water until it was up to his neck. Then he spun the bag over his head and hurled it as far out to sea as he could.

When he went back into the house to dry himself off, he was livid with cold. To warm up, he made another pot of coffee and drank it boiling.

✻

As he was driving towards the Palermo airport at Punta Raisi, his thoughts returned to the seagull he'd seen dancing and dying. For no real reason he'd always had the impression that birds were eternal, and whenever he happened to see a dead one he felt mildly wonderstruck, as if he was looking at something that should never have happened. He was almost positive that the gull he'd watched die had not been shot. Almost positive, that is, because it was possible that it had been struck by a single pellet of birdshot that didn't draw a drop of blood but was enough to kill it. Did seagulls always die like that, performing that sort of harrowing dance? He couldn't get the image of its death out of his head.

When he got to the airport, he looked up at the electronic arrivals board and had the nice and predictable news that the flight was more than an hour late.

How could you go wrong? Was there anything whatsoever in Italy that left or arrived at the scheduled time?

The trains ran late, the planes did too, the ferries required the hand of God to sail, the post we won't even mention, the buses actually got lost in traffic, public works projects were usually off by five to ten years, any law whatsoever took years before it was passed, trials in the courts were backed up, and even television programmes always started a good half-hour after the scheduled time . . .

Whenever Montalbano started to think about these things his blood boiled. But he really didn't want to be in a bad mood when Livia arrived. He had to find some distraction to make the extra hour pass.

The morning drive had whetted his appetite a little. Strange, since he never ate breakfast. He went to the airport bar, where there was a queue as long as at the post office on pension day. At last his turn came.

'A coffee and a *cornetto*, please.'

'No *cornetti*.'

'You've run out already?'

'No. The delivery's late today. We should have them in half an hour or so.'

Even the *cornetti* ran late!

He drank his coffee with a heavy heart, bought a newspaper, sat down, and began to read. All idle chatter and hot air.

The government chattered, the opposition chattered, the Church chattered, the Manufacturers' Association chattered, the trade unions chattered, and there was a welter of chatter about a famous couple who had split up, a photographer who had photographed something he wasn't supposed to, the richest, most powerful man in the country whose wife had written him a public letter chastising him for things he'd said to another woman, and endless chatter and natter about stonemasons falling like ripe pears from scaffolding, illegal aliens drowning at sea, pensioners with barely enough rags to cover their arses, and little children being raped.

The papers chattered everywhere and always about every problem in existence, but always idly, without it ever leading to any sort of understanding or concrete action...

Montalbano decided there and then that Article 1 of the Italian Constitution needed to be changed: 'Italy is a republic founded on selling drugs, systematic lateness, and useless chatter.'

Disgusted, he threw the newspaper into a bin, stood up, went out of the airport, and lit a cigarette. And saw seagulls flying very near the shore. Suddenly the seagull he'd seen dance and die came back to him.

Since there was still another half-hour before the flight arrived, he retraced on foot the road he'd driven in on until he was a few yards from the rocks. He stood there, relishing the scent of seaweed and salt and watching the birds pursue one another.

Then he went back to the airport. Livia's plane had just landed.

She appeared before him, beautiful and smiling. They hugged each other tight and kissed. They hadn't seen each other for three months.

'Shall we go?'

'I have to get my suitcase.'

The luggage, naturally, arrived an hour late amidst yells, curses, and protests. But they were lucky it hadn't been sent on to Bombay or Tanzania.

As they were driving back to Vigàta, Livia said: 'I reserved the hotel room in Ragusa for tonight, you know.'

*

The plan they'd made was to travel around for three days in the Val di Noto and visit the Sicilian baroque towns there, which Livia had never seen.

But it hadn't been an easy decision.

'Listen, Salvo,' Livia had said on the phone a week earlier, 'I've got four days off. What do you say I come down and we spend a little quiet time together?'

'Sounds wonderful.'

'I was thinking we could even do a little tour of Sicily, maybe to an area I'm not familiar with.'

'I think that's an excellent idea. Especially since there's not much to do at the station at the moment. Do you know where you'd like to go?'

'Yes. To the Val di Noto. I've never been there before.'

Damn! How did she get it in her head to go there, of all places?

'Well, it's certainly remarkable, I'll grant you that, but believe me, there are other places that—'

'No, I want to go to Noto, in particular. I'm told the cathedral is a pure marvel. Then we could push on to, I dunno, Modica, Ragusa, Scicli . . .'

'Nice itinerary, no doubt about it. But . . .'

'What, don't you think it's a good idea?'

'Well, in a general sense, yes, I think it's a great idea, absolutely. But we should probably inform ourselves first.'

'Of what?'

'Well, I wouldn't want them to be shooting.'

'What are you talking about? Shooting what?'

'I wouldn't want to run into a film crew shooting an episode of that television series just as we're walking around there . . . They film them around there, you know.'

'What the hell do you care?'

'What do you mean, what the hell do I care? And

what if I find myself face to face with the actor who plays me? ... What's his name – Zingarelli ...'

'His name's Zingaretti, stop pretending you don't know. Zingarelli's a dictionary. But I repeat: what do you care? How can you still have these childish complexes at your age?'

'What's age got to do with it?'

'Anyway, he doesn't look the least bit like you.'

'That's true.'

'He's a lot younger than you.'

Enough of this rubbish about age! Livia was obsessed!

He felt offended. What the hell did youth and age have to do with any of this?

'What the hell's that supposed to mean? Anyway, as far as that goes, he's totally bald, whereas I've got more hair than I know what to do with!'

'Come on, Salvo, let's not fight.'

And so, to avoid a quarrel, he'd let himself be talked into it.

*

'I'm well aware that you reserved a room. Why are you telling me this?'

'Because you'll have to come home from the office no later than four o'clock for us to make it there.'

'That's not a problem. I've only got a few documents to sign.'

Livia laughed.

'What's so funny?'

'Salvo, you say that as if this was the first time you—' She broke off.

'Come on, finish your sentence. The first time I what?'

'Never mind. Have you packed a suitcase, at least?'

'No.'

'Oh, great! It's going to take you two hours to pack, and at your normal cruising speed we'll be lucky to get to Ragusa before night!'

'Ah, "my cruising speed"! Aren't we witty today! How long does it take to pack a suitcase? I'll do it in half an hour!'

'Should I start packing it myself?'

'For heaven's sake, no!'

The one time he'd let her pack his bags, he'd found himself on the island of Elba with one brown shoe and one black one.

'What's that "for heaven's sake" supposed to mean?' Livia asked, sounding irritated.

'Nothing,' he said, having no desire to quarrel.

After a few minutes of silence, Montalbano asked: 'Do seagulls die in Boccadasse?'

Livia, who'd been staring at the road in front of her as though still resentful over the business of the suitcase, turned towards him with a look of astonishment and said nothing.

'Why are you looking at me like that? I simply asked you if seagulls die in Boccadasse.'

Livia kept staring at him without saying anything.

'Would you please answer me? Yes or no?'

'But don't you think that's a stupid question?'

'Can't you just answer me without assigning an IQ to my question?'

'I think they die in Boccadasse like anywhere else.'

'And have you ever seen one die?'

'I don't think so.'

'What do you mean, you don't think so? It's not a matter of doubt, you know. You've either seen one or you haven't! You can't go wrong!'

'Don't raise your voice. I've never seen one! Happy now? I've never seen one!'

'Now you're the one who's yelling!'

'But why do you ask me questions like that? You seem so strange this morning! Are you feeling all right?'

'I feel great! Like a god! Jesus motherfucking Christ, do I feel good! I've never felt better in all my life!'

'Don't talk in dialect and don't swear—'

'I'll talk however I want, OK?'

Livia didn't reply, and he fell silent. Neither said another word.

But how was it that they never failed to squabble over the slightest thing? And how was it that it never passed through either of their heads to draw the logical conclusion from the situation, which was to shake hands and break up once and for all?

They remained silent for the rest of the drive back to Marinella. Instead of leaving at once for the station, Montalbano felt like a shower. Maybe it would wash away the agitation that had come over him after quarrelling with Livia in the car. She, however, had locked herself in the bathroom upon arrival.

He took his clothes off and tapped discreetly at the door.

'What do you want?'

'Hurry up, I want a shower.'

'Just wait. I'm first.'

'Come on, Livia, I have to go to the office!'

'But you said all you have to do is sign some papers!'

'All right, but don't forget that I've just made a trip, Vigàta–Palermo, and back, to go pick you up! I need a shower!'

'And haven't I just come all the way from Genoa? Isn't that a little further? So I'm first!'

So now she's counting the miles?

He cursed the saints, looked for his trunks, put them on, and went down to the beach.

Although the sun was high in the sky by now, the sand under his feet was cool. The instant he got in the water, the cold nearly gave him a heart attack. The only solution was to start swimming at once, and vigorously.

After a good quarter of an hour of breaststroke, he floated on the surface.

In the sky there wasn't a bird to be seen anywhere, not for all the money in the world. As he lay there with his mouth open, a few drops of seawater slid down his face and into his mouth, between his palate and tongue. It tasted strange.

He brought a handful of water to his mouth. There was no doubt, the sea didn't taste the way it used to. It seemed to lack salt, and was bitter and nasty, like stale mineral water. Maybe that was why the seagulls . . . But then why did the mullets he feasted on at the trattoria still have the same delightful fragrance they'd always had?

As he was swimming towards the beach, he saw Livia sitting on the veranda in her dressing gown, drinking coffee.

'How's the water?'

'Stale.'

*

When he came out of the shower, he found Livia standing in front of him.

'What is it?'

'Nothing. Do you have to go to the station right away?'

'No.'

'Well, then . . .'

He understood. Hearing a sort of symphony orchestra strike up in his head, he squeezed her tight.

It was a beautiful way to make peace.

'Four o'clock, and I mean it!' she reminded him afterwards, accompanying him to the door.

*

'Get me Fazio right away,' he said to Catarella as he passed his post.

'He ain't onna premisses, Chief.'

'Has he called?'

'Nossir, Chief.'

'As soon as he gets in, tell him to come to my office.'

There was a veritable mountain of papers teetering on his desk. He felt disheartened. He was tempted to ignore it all. What could they do to him if he didn't sign them? The death penalty had been abolished, and even life sentences were on the way out. And so? Maybe with a good lawyer he could drag things out until his crime of refusal to apply his signature fell under the statute of limitations. There were even prime ministers who had benefited from this statute of limitations to dodge prosecution for much more serious crimes.

But then his sense of duty won.

TWO

Augello came in without knocking or even saying hello. He looked downcast.

'What's wrong, Mimì?'

'Nothing.'

'Come on, Mimì.'

'Leave me alone.'

'Come on, Mimì.'

'I spent the whole night arguing with Beba.'

'Why?'

'She says I don't earn enough and she wants to find a job. Actually, she's already been offered a good one.'

'And you're against it?'

'No. The problem is the kid.'

'I see. You mean, how can she work with the kid?'

'For her there's no problem. All taken care of. She wants to send him to nursery.'

'So?'

'Well, I'm against it.'

'Why?'

'He's too small. It's true he's old enough, but he's too small and I feel bad for him.'

'You think he'll be mistreated?'

'Of course not! He'd be treated just fine! But I feel bad for him anyway. I'm hardly ever at home. If Beba starts working, she'll go out in the morning and not come home till evening. And the kid'll think he's been orphaned.'

'Don't talk rubbish, Mimì. Being an orphan is something else altogether. I can tell you from experience, as you know.'

'Sorry. Let's change the subject.'

'Any news?'

'Nah. Dead calm.'

'Do you know why Fazio hasn't turned up yet?'

'No.'

'Listen, Mimì, have you ever seen a seagull die?'

'No.'

'This morning I watched one die right in front of the veranda.'

'Had it been shot?'

'I can't say.'

Augello stared at him. Then he stuck two fingers in the breast pocket of his jacket, pulled out his glasses, and put them on. 'What do you mean?'

'No, first you have to tell me why you put your glasses on.'

'To hear you better.'

'Do they have a hearing device built in?'

'No, I can hear just fine.'

'So why did you put your glasses on?'

'To see you better.'

'Oh, no you don't, Mimì, that's cheating! You said you put them on to hear me better! Hear, not see!'

'It's the same thing. If I can see you better, I can understand you better.'

'And what's to understand?'

'What're you getting at?'

'I'm not getting at anything, Mimì! I just asked you a simple question!'

'And since I know you well, I know where this simple question is going to lead.'

'And where's that?'

'To us starting an investigation into who killed that seagull! You'd be perfectly capable of it!'

'Don't talk crap!'

'Oh, no? And what about the time you found that dead horse on the beach? You made trouble for everyone until you were able to—'

'You know what I say to you, Mimì? Get the hell out of here and go and scratch your balls in your own office.'

*

He'd been signing papers upon papers for half an hour when the phone rang.

'Chief, 'at'd be a Mr Mizzica 'at wants a talk t'yiz poissonally in poisson.'

'On the phone?'

'Nossir, 'e's onna premisses.'

'Did he say what he wanted?'

'Says iss a quesshin o' trawlers.'

'Tell him I'm too busy and he should talk to Inspector Augello.' Then he changed his mind. 'Actually, no, I'll talk to him first.'

If Mr Mizzica dealt in trawlers, maybe he could tell him something about seagulls.

'I am Adolfo Rizzica, Inspector.'

As if Catarella would ever get a name right!

'Please sit down and tell me what I can do for you. But I should warn you that I've got barely five minutes. Just give me a general sense, and you can tell the rest to my second-in-command, Augello.'

Rizzica was about sixty and well dressed, with a polite and respectful demeanour. He had a salt-eaten face typical of a man of the sea. He sat on the edge of his chair, quite nervous. His forehead was beaded with sweat and he clutched a handkerchief in his hands. He kept his eyes lowered and couldn't make up his mind to begin talking.

'Mr Rizzica, I'm waiting.'

'I own five trawlers.'

'I'm glad to hear it. And so?'

'I think I can talk straight with you, so I'll get right to the point. One of these five boats seems suspicious to me.'

'Suspicious in what way?'

'Well, once or twice a week, this trawler comes in late.'

'I still don't understand. Comes in later than the others?'

'Yes, sir.'

'So where's the problem? Please try to be—'

'Inspector, normally I know where these guys piss, how much time they take to do it, and I'm always in touch with them via radiotelephone. And when they've finished, they tell me they're on their way in.'

'And so?'

'Even the captain of this boat, whose name is *Maria Concetta*—'

'The captain's a woman?'

'No, sir, he's a man.'

'So why does he have a woman's name?'

'It's the boat that has a woman's name, sir. The captain's name is Salvatore Aureli.'

'OK, and?'

'Captain Aureli will tell me he's coming in with the others, but then will put in an hour late, sometimes an hour and a half.'

'Does his boat have a slower engine?'

'No, sir, on the contrary.'

'So why's he coming in late?'

'That's the mystery, Inspector. I think the whole crew's in on it.'

'In on what?'

'That sea's full of traffic, Inspector. Worse than an autostrada, know what I mean?'

'No.'

'I think – but it's only what I think, mind you – I think he stops somewhere to load.'

'To load what?'

'Can't you guess?'

'Listen, Mr Rizzica, I haven't got time for guessing games.'

'In my opinion, Inspector, they're trafficking drugs. And if anyone finds out, I don't want any part of it.'

'Drugs? Are you sure?'

'Absolutely sure, no. But, you know . . .'

'And what sort of explanations has Aureli given for being late?'

'He comes up with a new story every time. Once it was because the engine seized up, another time the nets got caught—'

'Listen, perhaps it's best if you go at once and talk to Inspector Augello about all this. But first I'd like to ask you one question.'

'Of course.'

'Have you ever happened to see a seagull die?'

Hardly expecting such a question, Rizzica gave him a bewildered look. 'What's that got to do with—'

'It's got nothing do with it, nothing at all. It's just something I'm personally curious about.'

The man thought it over briefly.

'Yes, once, when I had only one trawler and was going on board, I saw a gull fall down dead.'

'Did it do anything before dying?'

The man grew even more bewildered. 'What was it supposed to do, write a will?'

Montalbano got irritated. 'Listen, Mizzica—'

'Rizzica.'

'—don't get clever with me! I asked you a serious question.'

'OK, OK, I'm sorry.'

'So, what did it do before it died?'

Rizzica thought about it for a minute.

'It didn't do anything, Inspector. It fell like a stone into the water and just floated there.'

'Ah, so it died at sea,' said Montalbano, disappointed.

If it fell into the water, there was no way it could have performed its dance.

'I'll show you into Inspector Augello's office,' he said, getting up.

*

Was it possible that nobody else had ever seen a seagull dancing as it died? Was he the only one? Who could he ask? The telephone rang. It was Livia.

'Did you know your fridge's empty?'

'No.'

'This is clearly an act of sabotage by your beloved

Adelina. You told her I was coming, and the woman, who obviously hates me, cleaned it out.'

'Good Lord, such strong words! She doesn't hate you, you just don't particularly like each other, that's all.'

'So you put me on the same level as her?!'

'Livia, for heaven's sake, let's not start! There's no need to make a big fuss over an empty fridge. You can come and have lunch with me at Enzo's trattoria.'

'And how will I get there? On foot?'

'All right, then, I'll come and pick you up.'

'How soon?'

'Jesus, Livia, I'll come and get you when it's time.'

'But can't you give me even a vague idea of when—'

'I said I don't know!'

'Listen, don't get up to your usual tricks, I won't stand for it!'

'And what are these usual tricks of mine?'

'When you say you'll be there at a certain time and you turn up three hours late.'

'I'll be extremely punctual.'

'But you haven't told me what time you—'

'Livia, stop! Are you trying to drive me insane?'

'You already are insane!'

He hung up. And less than thirty seconds later, the phone rang. He grabbed the receiver and yelled angrily: 'I am not insane! Understand?'

There was a slight pause, and then Catarella began to speak, voice quavering.

'Chief! I swear on my mortal soul an' dead body, I nivver tought you wuz insane! I nivver said it!'

'Cat, I was wrong, what is it?'

'Iss Fazio's wife is what it is.'

'On the phone?'

'Nossir, she's 'ere poissonally in poisson.'

'Show her in.'

Why had Fazio sent his wife? Couldn't he have just phoned if he was ill?

'Hello, Grazia. What's wrong?'

'Hello, Inspector. I'm so sorry to bother you, but—'

'No bother at all. What is it?'

'You tell me.'

Good God, what did that mean?

Grazia, to judge from her eyes, was worried and troubled.

Montalbano decided at once to try to find out more, in the hope of gaining some understanding and responding properly.

'Meanwhile, please sit down. You seem upset.'

'My husband went out last night at ten o'clock, after you called him. He said he had to meet you at the port. And I haven't heard from him since. Usually when he stays out all night he gives me a call. But this time he didn't, so I'm a little worried.'

Ah, so that's what this was about. But he hadn't called Fazio the night before. And they didn't have an appointment at the port. What on earth was the good man up to?

At any rate, the first thing to do was to calm the wife down. And thus began an Oscar-worthy performance. Montalbano let out a sort of groan and slapped himself loudly on the forehead.

'*Madonna mia!* I completely forgot! I'm so sorry, signora, but it totally slipped my mind!'

'What, Inspector?'

'Your husband told me to phone you, since he couldn't! And to think he'd repeated it to me so many times! And I, like an idiot—'

'Please don't say that, Inspector.'

'Good God, I'm so sorry to have made you worry so! But rest assured, Grazia, your husband is just fine. He's involved in a very delicate—'

'That's enough for me, Inspector. Thank you.'

She stood up and held out her hand.

Fazio's wife was a woman worthy of the man. Of few words and great dignity, she never, on the few occasions the inspector had eaten at their house (but what a terrible cook!), got involved in the two men's conversation when they discussed work-related matters.

'I'll see you out,' said Montalbano.

He accompanied her to the car park, still apologizing, and watched her get into her husband's car. Which meant that Fazio hadn't taken it to go wherever he'd gone.

He went back into the station and stopped in front of the cupboard that served as a switchboard room. He said to Catarella:

'Call Fazio for me on his mobile phone.'

Catarella tried twice in rapid succession.

'Iss off, Chief.'

'Then tell Inspector Augello to come to my office at once.'

'But 'e's still wit' Mr Mizzica.'

'Tell him to tell Mizzica to fuck off.'

What could have possibly happened to Fazio? he wondered, worried, entering his office.

Fazio had lied to his wife, telling her he had an appointment at the port. Why at the port, of all places? That might be the answer to everything, or it might mean nothing at all. He might have simply said the first thing that had come into his head.

The troubling thing was that he hadn't phoned his wife. And that must certainly have been because . . . because apparently he was in no condition to do so.

'*Be clearer, Montalbà,*' said Montalbano Two.

'*He doesn't want to be any clearer because he's afraid,*' Montalbano One cut in.

'*Of what?*'

'*Of the conclusions he's forced to draw.*'

'*And what are they?*'

'*That Fazio can't phone because he's being held prisoner by someone, or else he's injured or dead.*'

'*But why do you always have to imagine the worst?*'

'*What else can you imagine in this situation? That Fazio ran off with another woman?*'

Augello came in.

'What's the big rush?'

'Close the door and sit down.'

Augello obeyed.

'Well?'

'Fazio has disappeared.'

Mimì gawked at him, open-mouthed.

*

After talking for a quarter of an hour, they came to a conclusion. Which was that Fazio had clearly started an investigation on his own without telling anyone. He did get these sorts of brilliant ideas every once in a while. This time, however, he'd underestimated the danger, which seemed strange, given his experience, and had ended up in trouble.

There was no other possible explanation.

'We have to track him down by tomorrow at the very latest,' said Montalbano. 'I can probably keep his wife at bay until then, since she has a lot of faith in me, but sooner or later I'll have to tell her the truth. Whatever it is.'

'Where do you want me to start looking?'

'Let's assume the story about the port is true. You should start there.'

'Can I take someone with me?'

'No, it's better if you go alone. I don't want word to go around that we're looking for him. It might get back to the wife. If by this time tomorrow we haven't made any progress, then we'll get moving on a big scale.'

After Augello left, the inspector had an idea.

'Catarella, get someone to sit in for you for five minutes, then come into my office.'

'Straightaways, Chief.'

And indeed he appeared straightaways.

'Listen, Cat, I need you to give me a hand with something.'

Catarella's eyes began to sparkle with contentment, and he stood at attention.

'I'll even give yiz both 'ands, Chief.'

'Think hard before answering. There's no direct phone line in Fazio's office, right?'

'Right, sir.'

'Therefore every phone call that comes in for him has to pass through the switchboard, right?'

Catarella didn't reply, but twisted up his face.

'What's wrong?'

'Chief. Fazio's got a mobble phone. If summon happens a call 'im on 'is mobble phone, Fazio's mobble phone, I mean, that summon callin' don' go true the swishboard.'

'That's true. But let's just put that problem aside for now. Let's think only about the switchboard. I want you to tell me whether there've been any phone calls for Fazio in the last four or five days, from anyone who had never called before. Is that clear?'

'Poifickly, Chief.'

'Now I want you to sit down at my desk, take a pen and a sheet of paper, and write down every name you can remember. And in the meantime I'm going to go outside to smoke a cigarette.'

'I'm sorry, Chief, but I coun't do that.'

'You can't remember who called?'

'No, no, Chief, I can't sit atcher disk.'

'Why not? The chair's the same as any other.'

'Yessir, 'ass right, sir, but iss the ass, if you'll ascuse the 'spression, o' the poisson sittin' in the chair 'at makes the chair wha' it is.'

'All right, then just stay seated where you are.'

He went outside the building, smoked a cigarette while walking slowly around the car park, then went back inside.

THREE

Catarella handed him a sheet of paper. There were three names written on it. Locicciro (which must have been Lo Cicero); Parravacchio (only God knew what the real name was); and Zireta (here the error was slight: Ziretta).

'Only three?'

'No, Chief, there's four.'

'But you wrote only three names.'

'I din't write the fourth cuz I din't need to. Y'see how, 'tween Garavacchio an'—'

'Who you wrote as Parravacchio.'

'Iss not important. Y'see, how 'tween Saravacchio an' Zireta 'ere's a blank space?'

'Yes. What's it mean?'

'Blank, Chief. It means blank.'

'I don't get it.'

'Means the fourth poisson 'at called's name's Blank.'

Genius.

'Listen, wasn't Blanc arrested last week for fighting?'

'Yessir, Chief. An' Loccicciro was callin' cuz summon livin' onna floor above 'is floor's pissin' on 'im – if you'll pardon my lankwitch – every mornin' from the overlookin' balcony.'

'And do you know what Parravacchio wanted?'

'Nah. But Taravacchio's a rilitive o' Fazio's.'

'Between Parravacchio and Ziretta, do you know who called more often?'

'Yessir, 'twas Pinetta, but he's calling 'bout a application fer applyin' fer a passpott.'

Montalbano felt disappointed.

'But insofar as concerning the continuous pain-in-the-arse calls in continuosity, 'twas Mansella doin' the callin' till five days ago.'

'Is that Mansella with an *s* or a *z*?'

'Wit' a *s* like a *z*, Chief.'

'And did this Manzella go through the switchboard when he called Fazio?'

'Chief, Mansella call true the swishboard insofar as cuz Fazio's mobble phone's always busy. Or swished off. An' so he tol' me 'e's Mansella an' 'at I's asposta tell summon a tell Fazio 'at 'e's asposta call 'im, 'im bein' Mansella. Or ellis 'e's asposta toin 'is mobble phone on.'

'And did Fazio call him back?'

'I dunno, Chief. Insofar as cuz I's never present. If he called 'im back, 'twas wit a mobble phone.'

'I guess you don't remember the first time this Manzella called.'

'Wait a seccon', Chief.'

He went out of the room, then returned at a run, holding a black notebook. He started leafing through it. The pages were densely covered with names and numbers.

'What's that?'

'Chief, innytime innyone calls, I write down 'is name, who's they want, the day, anna zack time o' day.'

'Why?'

'Cuz ya nivver know.'

'But aren't they automatically registered?'

'Yessir, 'ass true, but I don' trust nuthin' attomattic. Who knows 'ow the attomattic feels about it! Awright, 'ere we are: Mansella calla foiss time tin days ago. Then 'e call ivry day till five days ago. A lass time 'e call tree times. 'E'z noivous. An' 'e tol' me a tell Fazio 'at 'e better toin 'is mobble phone on.'

'And then?'

'An' 'enn 'e din't call no more. But after 'twas Fazio allways askin' a' least twice a day if Mansella a call askin' fr'im. An' ivry time I say no, 'e says if 'e calls to put 'im true straightaways cuz iss a rilly important matter.'

'All right, thanks, Cat. You've been very helpful.'

'One more ting, Chief, if I mays.'

'Go ahead.'

'Wass' goin' on wit Fazio?'

'Nothing, just some sort of mistake, no need to worry.'

Catarella went out, not very convinced.

Montalbano took a deep breath and decided to do

something he really had no desire to do. Might as well start with the worst. He dialled Dr Pasquano's phone number.

'Hello, is the doctor in?'

'The doctor's busy.'

'Montalbano here. Please get him for me.'

'I'm sorry, Inspector, you'll have to excuse me, but I'm really not up to it. He's darker than a storm cloud this morning, and at the moment he's right in the middle of a post-mortem.'

Pasquano must have lost a lot of money playing poker at the club last night. When this happened, one was better off dealing with a starving polar bear.

'Maybe you know the answer to my question. Did any new bodies come in last night?'

'You mean fresh corpses? No.'

The inspector heaved a sigh of mild relief.

He got up, went out of the office, and passing by Catarella, told him:

'I'm off to Montelusa. I'll be back in a couple of hours. If Inspector Augello asks for me, tell him to call me on my mobile.'

✳

There were three hospitals and two private clinics in Montelusa. It used to be that all you had to do was phone them, tell them you were the police, and they would tell you anything about anyone. Then, with the advent of pain-in-the-arse privacy laws, if you didn't go in person and show your warrant card, they wouldn't tell you a damn thing. At any rate, Fazio wasn't in any of the three hospitals. Now came the hard part: the private clinics, whose concept of secrecy outdid even that of Swiss banks. How many fugitive Mafiosi had been operated on in them? The reception area of the first one Montalbano visited looked like the lobby of a five-star hotel. Behind a front desk so shiny it could have been used as a mirror were two women dressed in white, one young and the other older. He went up to the latter and donned a very serious face.

'I'm Inspector Montalbano, police,' he said, taking out his warrant card.

'How may I help you?'

'My men will be here in ten minutes. I want all the patients to remain in their rooms, and no visitors who are already here can leave.'

'Are you joking?'

'I have a search warrant. We are looking for a dangerous fugitive named Fazio who we believe was admitted here yesterday.'

The woman, who had turned pale as a ghost, reacted.

'But no one has been admitted here for the past two days! Look for yourself!' she said, turning her computer screen towards him.

'Listen, there's no point arguing! We have learned that the Materdei Clinic—'

'But this isn't Materdei!'

'It's not?'

'No! We're the Salus Clinic.'

'Oh my God, I'm so sorry. I've made a mistake. I'm terribly sorry. I'll be on my way, then. Ah, but one very important thing: you mustn't, under any circumstances, notify the Materdei.'

*

At the second clinic they actually threw him out. There was a head nurse of about sixty, at least six foot one, skinny as death and just as ugly, the spitting image of Olive Oyl.

'We don't accept wounded people off the street.'

'Fine, signora, but—'

'I'm not married.'

'Well, don't despair. You'll see, one day your prince will come.'

'Out!'

As he was getting back in his car, he heard someone call him. It was a doctor he knew. He explained the situation. His friend told him to wait outside, then returned five minutes later.

'We haven't had any new admissions for two days.'

What was going on? Was everyone bristling with good health, or did they simply not have enough money to pay the private clinics' bills? Whatever the case, he had to conclude that Fazio hadn't been hospitalized anywhere around there. But where had he gone to hide?

As he was driving back to Vigàta, his mobile rang. It was Mimì Augello.

'Salvo, where are you?'

'I was just in Montelusa making the rounds of the hospitals. There's no sign of Fazio anywhere. I'm on my way back.'

'Listen ... Maybe you should ...'

Montalbano understood immediately.

'Don't worry, he's not at the morgue, either. How about you? Got any news?'

'That's what I was calling about. Can you come to the port? I'll wait for you at the entrance.'

'Which one?'

'I'm just outside the southern gate.'

'I'll be right there.'

*

The southern gate, the one closest to the eastern jetty, where the inspector often went for a walk after he ate, was used mostly by the steady flow of cars and trucks about to board the ferry for Lampedusa. The ferry left at midnight. Once the season began, that area of the port was a bivouac of foreign kids waiting to board.

On either side of the enormous gate was a sort of sentry-box for the customs police on duty, who checked the comings and goings.

But at that hour of the morning, all was quiet. The

pandemonium of cars and passengers began around five p.m.

'At night this gate and the central one are closed. Only the northern gate stays open,' Mimì explained.

'Why's that?'

'Because that's the area of the port where the trawlers dock and leave and where the refrigerated warehouses and refrigerated trucks are. It's basically the hub for the sea-food business.'

'Well, if something has happened to Fazio, it happened at night.'

'That's my point.'

'Then why are we standing at the wrong gate?'

'It may be the wrong gate, but the Customs officer on duty, Sassu, was on the northern gate last night.'

'Did he see anything?'

'Come on, you can talk to him yourself.'

Sassu looked to be just over twenty, but he seemed to be a quick, intelligent kid.

'The fishing boats start to come in just after midnight,' he said. 'They unload, and then one part of the day's catch is immediately warehoused; another part is loaded onto the refrigerated trucks, which leave at once. There's usually a lot of bustle until about three in the morning. Afterwards, there's about an hour of calm. And it was just before four o'clock that I heard the shots.'

'How many?' Montalbano asked.

'Two.'

'Are you sure they were gunshots?'

'Not at all. It might have been a motorbike backfiring. And, in fact, just a few minutes later a large motorcycle drove by. And that reassured me at the time.'

'Was there a passenger on the back?'

'No.'

'And you didn't hear any cries or yells?'

'Nothing.'

'Were you able to tell where the shots were coming from?'

This time Sassu seemed less certain.

'It's strange,' he said softly.

'What's strange?'

'Now that I think about it . . . It couldn't have been a motorbike.'

'Why not?'

'There was an interval of a couple of seconds between the two shots. The first one sounded like it came from over by the slipway, but the second one was a lot further away, out past the second or third warehouse . . . If it was a motorbike, the two bursts should have come from the same spot.'

'Did it sound like someone chasing someone else trying to run away and firing at him?'

'Yeah, something like that.'

They thanked the Customs officer.

'I don't like the look of this,' Augello observed darkly.

'Let's go for a little walk,' the inspector said.

'Where to?'

'To the area between the slipway and the two warehouses.'

There were about ten refrigerated warehouses, in a row on the outer part of the central quay, which was a sort of arm jutting into the harbour. The trawlers would dock directly there, and once they'd unloaded their catch they would move inside the quay, where they would dock at their respective berths and their crews would disembark and go home to sleep.

Montalbano and Augello walked up and down the slipway as far as the second warehouse, eyes glued to the ground.

The road was a muddy mire, with deep ruts left by truck tyres. The warehouses were all closed except for the third one, which had a Ford Transit van in front of it with its doors open. Inside the warehouse one could see electrical cables, dials, knobs, and valves. Perhaps the refrigeration system had failed and was being repaired. Despite the van, there wasn't a living soul about.

'Let's go, we're not going to find anything here,' said Mimì. 'We're wasting our time. We would have to dig through the mud to find any clues. Anyway, the stink in the air is starting to get to me. I feel like I'm going to throw up.'

To Montalbano, however, that smell not only was not a stink, he actually liked it. It was the product of a combination of seaweed, rotting fish, unravelled cordage, seawater, and tar, with a light touch of diesel thrown in. Delicious, indeed exquisite.

At the very moment they'd given up hope and were about to go back to the office, Mimì saw something sparkle at the top of the slipway. It was an empty cartridge case that hadn't been buried in the mud because it had fallen onto a piece of rotten plank. He bent down, picked it up, and wiped it with his hand. It wasn't the least bit rusted or damaged. Clearly it had been there for only a few hours, not days or months.

'Now we know for certain that it wasn't a motorcycle,' Montalbano concluded.

'At a glance, I'd say a 7.65,' said Augello. Then he asked: 'What should we do with this cartridge case?'

'Make soup.'

'What's that supposed to mean?'

'Mimì, how do you expect that cartridge case to help us? All it gives us is confirmation that a gun was fired. For the moment, it can't tell us anything else.'

After hesitating for a moment, Augello put it in his pocket.

Montalbano, having stopped, made no sign of resuming his walking.

He was thinking, head bent as he stared at the tops of his shoes. He had a cigarette between his lips but had forgotten to light it. Mimì stood there in silence. Then the inspector started talking, but rather than talking to Augello, he was thinking out loud.

'So they fired the first shot at Fazio – assuming it was Fazio – as he was going back towards the northern gate. Apparently he'd already finished doing whatever it was he had to do in the area of the warehouses and was now heading out of the port, but someone was waiting for him here and fired at him.'

'But why would they wait till he was at the slipway?' Mimì asked. 'It's the most dangerous spot because it's the closest to the gate where there's always a Customs agent.'

'They had no choice. Say they grabbed him and killed him in front of one of the warehouses. If they didn't get rid of the body really quickly, they would have been forced to leave it there. But once the corpse was discovered, we definitely would have searched the warehouses. Which they didn't want. The slipway, on the other hand, is a no-man's-land. Everyone who docks at this quay is forced to pass that way. It would be like shooting him on the main street in town.'

'At any rate, they didn't get him with the first shot.'

'Right. But then Fazio realizes he can't keep running towards the gate. His path is barred by the man who shot at him. So what does he do?'

'What does he do?'

'He turns tail and runs straight back the way he came, that is, towards the warehouses.'

'But that's even worse!'

'Why?'

'Because the road that passes in front of the warehouses ends at the sea! There's no access to the quay. Therefore he wouldn't have been able to escape his pursuer. There was no way out. He ran straight into his own trap.'

'But he knew exactly what the situation was at that moment, whereas we don't.'

'What do you mean?'

'Maybe there were some warehouses still open where he could ask for help. The fact is, as the Customs officer told us, they fired a second shot at him when he'd reached the second or third warehouse. And the fact that he didn't hear any other shots is a bad sign.'

'Meaning?'

'Meaning that that second shot may have wounded or killed him.'

'Jesus Christ!' Augello cried out.

'But it's also possible that Fazio, seeing there was no way out, put his hands up and let them capture him.'

'Listen, what if we got a search warrant for the warehouses?' Augello proposed.

'A waste of time.'

'Why on earth?!'

'If they killed him, they certainly wouldn't have kept the body. And even if he was wounded or captured, they couldn't keep him in a cold-storage facility for more than a couple of hours, or he'd turn stiffer than a stockfish.'

'OK, but if he's dead, where'd they put the body?'

'I think I have an idea. Want to hear it?'

'Of course.'

'In the sea, Mimì. Well ballasted.'

'What the hell are you saying?'

'It's just an idea, Mimì, no need to get upset. Try to think. If they did in fact kill him, throwing him into the sea was the easiest and safest thing to do. I'm convinced there was no way they could hide the body in one of the warehouses. Even if most of the heavy work was already done at that time of day, there had to be a few people still about. It would have been too risky. Trust me, we should stop thinking about it.'

'All right.'

'Tell you what. Call the commissioner. Tell him half the story. Actually, no. Don't tell him anything about Fazio. Tell him we need to recover a weapon that fell into the water. Get him to send you two frogmen.'

'Sorry, but what if he asks me whose weapon it is?'

'Tell him it's mine.'

'And how did it end up in the water?'

'Through a hole in the back pocket of my trousers.'

'And what if he says not to bother? That it's not worth the trouble?'

'Tell him it'll be his responsibility.'

'What'll be his responsibility?'

'Explain to him that when my gun fell out, there were a lot of people around. And that if one of them felt like getting wet, they might recover the weapon and use it.'

Mimì Augello stepped away and started talking on his

mobile phone. It was a long call, then he started shaking his head and walking back towards Montalbano. He held out the phone.

'He wants to talk to you,' he said.

'Montalbano! What the hell is going on?'

'I'm sorry, Mr Commissioner, it's all because of this hole in—'

'This is sheer lunacy! These things only happen to you! A hole! And what if the weapon had fallen onto a crowded street and gone off?'

'I never keep it loaded, sir.'

'Look, Montalbano, I can't request two frogmen for something as silly as this!'

'If you prefer, I can jump into the sea myself. I can stay underwater for a very long time, you know.'

'Montalbano, every time I talk to you it's an ordeal! Give me Augello again.'

Mimì talked for another five minutes, then signed off and said to Montalbano: 'I managed to persuade him.'

*

The inspector's hunch turned out to be wrong.

By the time the sun started to set, the two frogmen, who'd worked for three hours straight, hadn't found a thing.

Or, more precisely, they'd found everything but the kitchen sink, even a baby buggy and a suitcase full of jars of tomato sauce. Luckily, however, no dead body.

'So much the better,' said Montalbano.

Meanwhile, dozens of people had gathered and were craning their necks, looking on, talking, laughing, asking questions that nobody answered. Montalbano felt only contempt for them.

Then a man approached him and said he was the owner of one of the warehouses.

'Sorry to bother you, Inspector. But I need to know what we're supposed to do.'

'What you're supposed to do about what?'

'About the fishing boats.'

'But there isn't a single one here.'

'In about two hours they're going to start coming in.'

'So?'

'With the frogmen working right in front of the warehouses, they won't be able to dock and unload.'

'Don't worry. We'll be finished in fifteen minutes.'

'Mind telling us what you're looking for?' the man asked in dialect.

It put them on common ground.

'Sure. My watch. It fell in the water this morning.'

'They said you dropped your gun.'

'I was wrong. I always get the two confused.'

FOUR

When Mimì and the inspector gathered back at the station, it was almost nine p.m. Neither had found the time to eat anything. Or, more precisely, they could have taken an hour or so to eat something, had they wanted, but the truth was that neither of them had felt like it.

'Did Fazio ever show up, by any chance?'

'Nossir, Chief.'

They went into Montalbano's office.

'Have a seat, Mimì. Let's think for another five minutes. Shall I send for some coffee?'

'Good idea.'

Montalbano picked up the phone.

'Cat, could you go and get us a couple of coffees at the bar? Thanks.'

They eyed each other.

'You first,' said Mimì.

'It's clear by now they've got Fazio. Whether dead or alive is another question.'

'Well, he wasn't in the sea, at any rate.'

'But that still doesn't mean we know he's alive.'

'Agreed. But if they got him with the second shot, the one fired around the warehouses, where'd they put him?'

'Mimì, we're unable to come up with an answer for one simple reason. Namely, we don't know what happens when the trawlers come in, how much time they take to unload, at what time they leave the warehouses to go to their berths, how long the refrigerated trucks stay there before leaving with their loads of fish . . . To put it simply, what sort of activity is there at that time of the night?'

'The Customs officer said he'd heard the shots just before four, and that between three and four o'clock, everything had been quiet.'

'Fine, but what does "quiet" mean? That there wasn't a soul around? That's not possible; there must still be some people about, even at that hour. In fact, the Customs agent said he saw a motorcycle drive past after he'd heard the two shots. So there must still have been somebody there.'

Suddenly the door flew open and crashed against the wall. Mimì and the inspector leapt out of their chairs. Augello cursed under his breath. Catarella appeared, holding a little tray with both hands, his right foot still in mid-air.

'Sorry 'bout that, 'spectors, I kinda miscaliculated the strinth o' my kick.'

He set the tray down on the desk.

'Listen, Cat, did anyone call for Fazio today?' the inspector asked him.

Catarella thrust a hand into his pocket and pulled out his little black notebook. Licking the tip of his index finger, he started skimming through it.

Augello gawked at him in astonishment.

'Less see. Blank an' Loccicciro called.'

'But not the others?'

'Sarravacchio came poissonally in poisson.'

'So the only one who didn't call for him was Manzella.'

''Ass azackly azack, Chief.'

'I haven't understood a damn thing,' said Augello as Catarella was leaving.

The coffee was good. And the inspector told him about Manzella's phone calls.

'So,' said Mimì, 'in your opinion, Manzella didn't call today because he knows exactly what happened to Fazio.'

'It's fairly likely.'

'So what do we do now?'

'You're going to go home to Beba and the kid.'

'And you?'

'I'm going to rest a little here and then go back to the quay to see how the fishing business operates.'

He was leaving the room when the phone rang.

'Chie f? 'At'd be the newsman Zito onna line.'

'Put him on . . . Hello, Nicolò, how are you doing? Haven't heard from you for a while. How's the wife?'

'Fine, thanks. Listen, are you going to be at the office a little longer?'

'Actually, no, I was just about to go out.'

'Home?'

'No. Why do you want to know?'

'No reason, just to make conversation.'

'No, Nicolò, you're not being straight with me. What is it?'

'I just wanted to know something. Tell you what. If you're in a hurry, put Fazio on. I'll ask him.'

'He's not here.'

'Did he go home?'

'I don't know.'

'All right, I'll try calling him anyway.'

'No!'

Damn, he'd said it too loudly!

When Zito spoke, he seemed to falter. 'Sorry, but what—'

'Look, Nicolò. The fact is that his wife . . . isn't feeling so good and he's really worried . . . You know?'

'I understand. All right, good night.'

Had Nicolò Zito actually swallowed the whopper he'd just fed him?

Whatever the case, that phone call from his friend and Free Channel newsman had seemed a little strange to him, no doubt about it.

*

When he got to the quay, a few trawlers were already tied up in front of the warehouses and unloading their catch. The floodlights were all on. He could see, in the distance, at the mouth of the harbour, the navigation lights of the other trawlers coming in.

A veritable babble of shouts, curses, and commands could be heard above the din of the boats' diesel motors, the trucks' engines, and the continual rumble of the freezers.

In the small spaces between one warehouse and the next, which were a kind of narrow alleyway, the inspector discovered a great hubbub of makeshift fish stalls, with crates of fish being sold by the crews of the trawlers. And it wasn't the discards they were selling, but the share due to the members of each boat. The buyers, after a sort of tug-of-war of bargaining, loaded the crates onto scooters or three-wheeled Ape vans and drive off. They must have been restaurant owners or employees, who were thus assured not only of having fresh fish, but of paying half what they would have paid at the market in town.

Montalbano remembered the trawler owner who had come to the station. What was his name? Ah, yes, Rizzica. He had to be around there somewhere.

He stopped a municipal police officer he saw carrying a box of fish. It had to have been his payoff for closing an eye to the makeshift market in the alleyway.

'I'm Inspector Montalbano, and I'd like to know—'

The cop turned pale.

'I paid for this fish! I swear!' he said, voice quavering.

'I don't doubt it for a minute.'

'So what do you want, then?'

'I want to know where I can find Mr Rizzica.'

'You can find Rizzica in one of his warehouses.'

'And which ones are they?'

'Numbers three, four, and the last one.'

'Thanks.'

'Glad to be of service!' said the officer, clearly relieved and practically running away, terrified that Montalbano might change his mind and demand that he explain how he came by that box of fish.

In front of the open door of warehouse number three was the same Ford van as that morning. Montalbano went inside and immediately saw Rizzica.

He was talking with an air of concern to a man in overalls. The moment he saw Montalbano, however, he came towards him, hand outstretched.

'Let's go outside,' he said.

Apparently he didn't want to talk in the presence of the man in overalls. They stopped in a sort of archway to one side of the quay that smelled of shit and piss old and new, which was why there wasn't anyone in the vicinity.

'Did you come here because of my complaint?'

'No. Did you file a formal complaint with Inspector Augello?'

'No, sir, not formally. But it's still a complaint.'

'Have your boats come in?'

'No, there's another hour and a half to go.'

'And the one that's always late, the . . . what was its name?'

'The *Maria Concetta*? No, today's her day off. But tonight it would be better if they were all late.'

'Why?'

'Because one of my warehouses has been out of order since yesterday. The refrigeration system is down. You have no idea how much money it's cost me. I had to throw all the fish back into the sea. The electrician says they'll have to order a replacement part from Palermo. And just to rub it in, the two boats coming in now are full of fish; they had a really good catch today. I'm going to have to get the third warehouse up and running, the one I usually use only for—'

'But didn't you say you had five trawlers?'

'Yes, sir.'

'How come you've only got two out?'

'I have 'em working in shifts, Inspector. Three go out, and two rest. An' vice versa.'

'I see.'

'Listen, I have to go back inside. But about that thing I mentioned to you, Inspector Augello knows the whole story. He can answer your questions.'

'No problem. Listen, what did you say was the name of the captain of the *Maria Concetta*?'

'Aureli. Salvatore Aureli.'

'One more thing. Do you remember the names of the rest of the crew?'

'I told 'em to Inspector Augello.'

'Tell me too.'

'Totò Albanese, Gaspano Bellavia, Peppe Dima, Gegè Fragapane, 'Ntonio Zambito, an' two Tunisians whose names I don' remember right now but I gave 'em to Inspector Augello.'

No Manzella. For a brief moment, he'd been hoping.

*

After three in the morning, the hustle and bustle had wound down for the most part. The trawlers were no longer tied up in front of the warehouses, by now they were all at their berths inside the port. The refrigerated trucks had also all left. The great main doors of the warehouses were all locked, except for number three, where the electricians were still trying to repair the failure. But . . .

But the road wasn't entirely deserted. There were still five or six people about, talking and arguing. Two of them had even raised their voices and were about to get into a fight. If it was always this way at this hour of the night, someone must surely have heard or even witnessed Fazio running away as someone ran after him, firing his gun.

Hadn't the Customs officer said that after hearing the two shots he'd seen a high-powered motorcycle drive past? So therefore there had been at least one witness! But these were the kind of people who would never talk, Montalbano was absolutely certain of that.

All at once he felt a crushing fatigue descend upon him, so great that for a moment his knees buckled.

There was no point in wasting any more time. He decided he would go to the commissioner in the morning and tell him the whole story, so they could officially begin the search. He threw in the towel. The crucial thing was that the more time went by, the worse it was for Fazio, assuming he was still alive.

'Montalbano!'

He turned around and found himself face to face with Nicolò Zito.

'How did you know I was here?'

'Augello told me. I rang him at home after trying without success to contact you.'

'What's going on?'

'I have to talk to you.'

'So talk.'

'Shall we go to my car?'

He'd parked it near the slipway. The early morning wind was biting hard and Montalbano, exhausted, famished, and worried as he was, began to shiver from the cold.

Once inside the car, he leaned his head back against the seat and closed his eyes.

He reopened them when he smelled coffee. Zito had shoved the cap of a hot thermos under his nose. The inspector rejoiced.

ANDREA CAMILLERI

'How long has it been since Fazio went missing?' the journalist asked.

Montalbano choked on his coffee. Zito slapped him twice on the back to help.

'Who told you?'

'I got a phone call and then you confirmed it for me.'

'I did?!'

'You certainly did. When you shouted "No!" so that I wouldn't call Fazio's house. That pretty much sealed it for me. I realized then and there that something wasn't right. What was he investigating?'

'That's just it, Nicolò. I don't know. He was working on his own, you see. And hadn't told anyone. Who called you?'

'I can't tell you. He called me and said he thought he'd seen Fazio in a bad situation.'

'In what sense?'

'His head was wrapped, as if to cover a wound.'

'Was he alone?'

'No. But let me finish. Since he wasn't sure it was actually Fazio, this gentleman wanted me to find out. Which I did, and so I called him back on his mobile and told him I had the impression that you had confirmed his hunch, however indirectly. And so he kept telling me to call him back in two hours.'

'Sorry to interrupt, but why didn't you contact us straightaway?'

'I'll tell you in a second. So I called back two hours

54

later and he gave me precise directions as to where we could find him, so that he could explain everything. Do you want to go?'

'Of course. Where is it?'

'Near Rivera. An hour and a half's drive away.'

'All right, let's get moving. Would you please tell me why you didn't call us?'

'Because he's a fugitive, Salvo.'

So why would a fugitive from justice worry about the fate of a cop? There was no point in asking any questions, however. Zito would never divulge the informer's name.

There was, however, one good thing in all this: Fazio was still alive.

'What did you tell Augello?'

'That I urgently needed to talk to you.'

'Did you mention that it had to do with Fazio?'

'No.'

Should he phone Mimì to tell him about the new development? No, it was probably best to let him sleep. And at the sound of that word in his mind, as if by sudden contagion, he closed his eyes automatically. And fell asleep.

*

He was awakened by the silence.

He was alone. It was daylight. The car was stopped on a track in the open country. But all around him was not what you could really call country, only desolate, deserted land. A few stunted trees where it was impossible to tell what, if any, fruit they had ever borne, a few clumps of wild grass as tall as a man, thickets of sorghum, and a sea of white stones.

It was a *chiarchiaro*, as they called it in Sicilian, a hill of stone, a godforsaken place where you couldn't grow anything and it was dangerous even to walk, since at any moment you could find yourself sinking into a hole that would widen into a great fissure plunging deep into the ground.

Montalbano knew that *chiarchiari* were cemeteries of nameless bones, the favourite burial sites of the Mafia. When they wanted to make someone disappear, they would take him to the edge of a hole, shoot him, and let him fall inside. Or else they would spare themselves the bullets, and just shove him into the chasm still alive, and the victim would die during the fall, crashing against the rocks, or if he reached the bottom, he could cry and yell all he wanted, and nobody would ever hear him. He would die slowly, of hunger and, above all, thirst.

To the right, about ten yards from the lane, was a tumbledown little one-room house, a white dice that looked merely like a rock a bit larger than the rest. Tumbledown, perhaps, but with the door closed. Maybe Nicolò was inside, talking to the fugitive.

Montalbano decided to stay in the car. He searched his pockets. There were only three cigarettes left in the pack. He lit one and rolled down the window. He didn't hear any birds singing.

Then, when he'd nearly finished the cigarette, the door of the dice opened and Zito appeared, motioning to him to come out and approach.

'He's ready to tell you everything, but there's one problem.'

'What?'

'He doesn't want you to see his face.'

'So what should we do?'

'I have to blindfold you.'

'Is this some kind of joke?'

'No. If you're not blindfolded, he won't talk.'

'I'll make him talk.'

'Don't talk rubbish, Salvo. You and I are unarmed, and he's got a gun. Come on, don't be an idiot.'

And Nicolò pulled an enormous handkerchief out of his pocket, red and green, like a peasant's.

Despite the circumstances, Montalbano started laughing.

'Is that really your normal handkerchief?'

'Yes. I've been using this kind for a while. Sinusitis.'

The inspector let himself be blindfolded and led into the cottage.

'Good morning, Inspector Montalbano,' said a middle-aged voice, rather deep and well mannered.

'Good morning to you.'

'I'm sorry I've made you come all this way, and I'm sorry I've made you wear a blindfold, but it's better if you don't know who I am.'

'Let's drop the politeness crap,' the inspector said. 'Just tell me what you have to tell me.'

'The other morning, probably around six o'clock, I was in the vicinity of Monte Scibetta. Do you know the area of the dry wells?'

'Yes.'

'I was in a car and was passing by the drinking trough, which used to have water in it. There were three people there, and one of them was sitting on the edge of the trough. The other two were on his right. The seated man had a bandage over his forehead, and his shirt was all stained with blood. Then one of the two punched him in the face, and he fell into the trough. But I'd already recognized him. Or at least I think I had. He looked to me like Signor Fazio.'

'Are you sure about that?'

'Quite sure.'

'Then what?'

'I kept on driving, and in the mirror I saw them pulling him back out.'

'And what did you do after that?'

'I had to get away from Monte Scibetta, and fast, because I'd found out that the carabinieri were coming after me. So I thought the best place to hide was here. But before I got here, I called Mr Zito.'

'How do you know each other?'

'Never mind about that,' Nicolò's voice said behind him.

'All right, go on.'

'First of all, I wanted confirmation that it was actually Fazio.'

'And when you knew for certain, why did you want Zito to tell me about your phone call?'

'Because once, with my son, Fazio showed he was an honourable man.'

'Why, in your opinion, did they take Fazio all the way out to Monte Scibetta?'

'I'm sorry, but I don't know why or where they grabbed him.'

'They almost certainly wounded and captured him at the port of Vigàta.'

'Ah,' said the stranger.

But he didn't speak.

'And so?' Montalbano asked, feeling agitated.

'Inspector, if they took him all the way out there, it was to throw him into one of those dry wells. They want to make him disappear. It would have taken them too long to bring him all the way out here to the *chiarchiaro*.'

It was the very answer he'd feared.

Now there was no more time to waste.

'Good luck, Mr Nicotra, and thanks,' said the inspector.

'But . . . how did you know it was me?'

'For one thing, I first heard your story a long time ago from Zito himself, who's been your friend since your schooldays. And then, when you said Fazio had treated your son honourably . . . well, I just put two and two together. Thanks again.'

FIVE

Once outside the dice, he removed the handkerchief covering his eyes and started running towards the car, with Zito following behind.

'Come on, hurry up!'

'Where are we going?' the newsman asked.

'To Monte Scibetta. We haven't a minute to lose!'

'Stop and think for a second, Salvo. Hour after hour has passed since he saw him there—'

'Oh, I'm thinking all right, don't you worry about that.'

'By now whatever they were going to do to Fazio, they've already done.'

'Yes, but he may still be alive. Maybe gravely wounded, but still alive. Do you know where the dry wells are?'

'Yes.'

'How far from here?'

'About two hours.'

'Let's go, and in the meantime give me your mobile.'

He called Augello, who was still asleep. But as soon as Montalbano told him what he'd found out, he woke up in a hurry.

'And you, Nicolò, should tell your friend Nicotra to turn himself in,' the inspector said to Zito when he'd finished.

'Do you know how many times I've told him that? It's hopeless. The idea of ending up in jail drives him crazy. If there's such a thing as incompatibility with prison life, he's got it. And two murders are still two murders.'

'OK, but he would have every mitigating circumstance in the book. For us, a cheating wife is the best mitigation there is. If you're being cheated on, you can even commit a massacre if you want, and still get off easy. What? You mean you caught your wife in bed with your brother and you didn't shoot them on the spot? What kind of man are you? Don't you know that with a jury made up of people with a sense of Honour, Family, Duty, and Womanly Virtue, Nicotra would surely be acquitted?'

*

They'd arranged to meet at the dried-up drinking trough. But when they got there, Augello and his men were nowhere to be seen.

'What the fuck are they doing?' Montalbano asked out loud, upset.

'Well,' Zito said, trying to calm him down, 'it's going to take a little time for him to do what you asked him.'

The inspector lit a cigarette. Luckily he'd found a cafe-tobacconist open in Rivera and had bought three packs, just to be safe.

The first to arrive were four firemen with a large engine equipped with a crane. Apparently Augello had clearly explained to them the work they would have to do, which was to go down into wells that had long run dry but were very deep.

'We're ready,' said the head fireman. 'Shall we go in?'

His name was Mallia and he'd listened almost distract-edly while the inspector reviewed the situation for him.

'We have to wait until my deputy gets here,' said Montalbano.

'Well, we're going to go ahead anyway and check things out. That'll save us a little time. We'll meet back up at the first well.'

'Do you know where they are?'

'Of course, just over a quarter of a mile from here. A couple of years ago I pulled a corpse out of one,' said Mallia.

A good start is the best of guides, as the poet said. Without anyone noticing, Montalbano superstitiously touched his balls to ward off bad luck.

At last Mimì arrived. A squad car came up behind him, with Gallo at the wheel, accompanied by Galluzzo and a young new officer, Lamarca, who seemed a bright, alert kid.

*

The three wells had been dug some thirty years ago, about a hundred yards apart, and were linked by a sort of narrow goat track. The land, about thirty hectares, had belonged for generations to the Fradella family, who, though good farmers, had never been able to grow a single tree there, or plant a square metre of any kind of plant whatsoever. It was useless land, all of it. Since legend had it that long ago brigands had raped and killed a poor peasant girl there, everyone believed that the land yielded nothing because it was cursed. And so the Fradellas summoned a hermit from Trapani province who knew how to fight the devil. Not even he was able to make so much as a blade of grass grow. The ground was sterile because it was arid, but perhaps only a little water would suffice to change everything. Then, about thirty years ago, Joe Fradella returned from America, where he owned a ranch, and he explained to his relatives that he knew an extraordinary diviner who could find water even in the middle of the Sahara desert. And he brought the diviner from America, at his own expense. The moment the diviner took a little walk around the area, he said: 'There's a sea under here!'

And so the Fradellas dug the first well, and about a hundred feet down the water started coming up nice and fresh. They dug another two, and within about two years, the land, irrigated by a round-the-clock system of pipes and canals, started to turn green. And whatever they planted there grew. In short, those thirty hectares became a sort of paradise on earth. Then the regional government decided to build a new high-speed road between Monte-lusa and Trapani. A public works project of great import-ance, the politicians said. The road was to pass straight through Monte Scibetta, and so they dug a tunnel that pierced the mountain from one end to the other. But once the tunnel was finished, everything else came to an end, too. That is, the high-speed road was never made, because the only thing that moved at high speed in the whole affair was the money allocated for it, which raced straight into the pockets of the contractors and local Mafia, and overnight, the water under the Fradellas' land, which was right up against the mountain, disappeared. The hole created by the tunnel had shifted the aquifer. And so the land went back to being what it had always been: arid and unproductive.

Since then, the dry wells had been used as convenient, anonymous tombs.

*

After the fireman had been lowered into the first well, duly strapped and attached to a winch, and found nothing, all the men and equipment moved on to the second well. There, the fireman had descended about twenty yards when he signalled that he wanted to be pulled back out.

'But he didn't go down to the bottom,' the inspector observed.

'Apparently there's a problem,' said Mallia.

When he'd returned to the top, the fireman said: 'I need a mask.'

'Is there not enough air down there?'

'There's enough air, but there's a terrible smell of rotting flesh.'

Montalbano felt as if he'd been punched in the stomach. He turned pale and didn't even have the strength to speak. He felt like throwing up. Augello spoke in his stead.

'Did you see ... whether ...'

'I didn't see anything. I only smelled.'

Noticing the change in Montalbano, Mallia intervened.

'It's not necessarily a human body, you know. It could easily be a sheep or a dog ...'

The fireman put on a mask and went back down. Mimì took Montalbano by the arm and pulled him aside.

'What's wrong with you? That can't be Fazio.'

'Why not?'

'Because his body wouldn't have had time to ... to be in that condition.'

Augello was right, but that didn't prevent Montalbano from continuing to feel a sort of inner trembling.

'Why don't you go sit in the car and rest a little? If there's any development, I'll come and get you.'

'No.'

He would never have managed to sit still. He needed to walk, maybe even around the well like a donkey attached to a millstone, as the others looked on with concern.

The fireman came up again.

'There's a body.'

Despite Augello's words, Montalbano felt a wave of nausea overwhelm him. As he leaned against a car, vomiting up his soul, he heard the fireman add:

'From the look of it, I'd say it's been there for at least four or five days.'

'We have to pull it out,' said the chief.

'That's not going to be easy,' the fireman observed.

Montalbano meanwhile had recovered somewhat from the malaise that had come over him. He'd felt a sort of electrical current run through his body from his brain down to the tips of his toes, and a bitter, acidic taste like regurgitation in his mouth. But if the body had been dead for four or five days, then Augello was right, it couldn't be Fazio. Except that this logical, reassuring consideration had only come afterwards, after the fright had already done its damage. All the same, Fazio's disappearance was eating him alive. He would have given anything, his money and his health, to find him.

'Have you got the right equipment for pulling him up?' he asked Mallia.

'Of course.'

'Then, Mimì, inform the prosecutor, Forensics, and Dr Pasquano.'

'Can we start right away, or do we have to wait for them to get here?' the fire chief asked.

'It's better to wait. Meanwhile we can go and have a look at the third well.'

'Are you thinking the person we're looking for is not the one we found?'

'At this point I'm absolutely certain.'

'But—'

'You have a problem with that?' the inspector asked, immediately turning defensive. He wasn't in the mood for any disagreement.

'No,' said Mallia. 'I didn't mean in any way to . . . Listen, we can go and check the third well, just not right now, but as soon as we've pulled out the body in this one. Moving the equipment and setting it up again is tiring and complicated, you see. Do you understand?'

He understood. With a tugging heart, and against his will, he understood.

'OK, all right.'

Zito, who'd been standing aside the whole time, came up to him. He realized the situation his friend was in. He knew what kind of relationship Montalbano and Fazio had.

'Salvo, can I call the studio?'

'Why?'

'If it's all right with you, I'd like to have someone cover this. It's important for us.'

He did owe Nicolò a good turn, by way of thanks. If not for him, he would still be searching for Fazio around the port.

'Go ahead.'

Alone, he started walking along the footpath that led to the third well. It went uphill, and after barely ten steps he was out of breath. He was too tired, and his concern for Fazio raged in his mind like a furious wind, preventing him from putting his thoughts in order, from thinking with the least bit of logic. He wasn't just exhausted; he still felt scared.

He was waiting, at any moment, to hear some bad news or to see, with his own eyes, what he could never put into words. At last he came to the third well. On the ground beside the opening there were still some rusted remains of what must have once been a large suction pump.

He sat down on the crumbling wall of the well to rest. The sun beat down hard, and the day had turned hot, but he was in a cold sweat. The ground all round the well was a sort of fine dust like sand, and he noticed some shoeprints on the surface. But since it seldom rained, and there wasn't much wind in that dead land, he was unable to determine whether they were recent or old. Then he rolled over onto his stomach and gazed into the well. Total darkness. No, they needed the fireman to go down.

But at any rate, if Fazio had ended up in there, there was a slight chance he might still be alive.

As the inspector walked back towards the firemen and his own men, he had an idea, and it seemed like a good one. He pulled Mimì aside.

'Listen, Mimì, the fire chief and I agreed that after they pull the body out, we'll go and check the third well.'

'Yeah, he told me.'

'If, as I'm hoping, Fazio's not in there, I want us to stay behind after everybody else leaves.'

'To do what?'

'What do you mean, to do what? To look for Fazio. I'm positive he's around here somewhere.'

'What makes you think that?'

'Fazio was wounded at the port, right? Then they put him in a car and brought him here, right? Once he was here, it's not like they treated him so well, you know, they kept on punching him, right? Therefore, if they didn't kill him and get rid of the body, then Fazio is somewhere around here, still wounded, because it would make no sense for them to put him back in the car and take him back to the port.'

'But what do you think we can do?'

'As soon as we've taken care of this corpse, I want you to get in the car, go straight to the commissioner, and tell him everything. We have to organize a large search party.'

'All right. And what about you?'

'Gallo and I, together with Galluzzo and Lamarca, are going to start looking around.'

'OK.'

*

The travelling circus that normally came together whenever there was a killing took two hours to arrive on the scene from Montelusa. The first to straggle in were the Forensics team, who began taking a few of the thousands of photographs, most of them useless, that they usually took on these occasions. This time they concentrated on the rim of the well and environs. Since Vanni Arquà, the chief of Forensics whom Montalbano didn't like one bit, wasn't present, the inspector went up to the man who was giving orders and told him that it might be a good idea to inspect the drinking trough very carefully, as there could be blood stains on it.

'But how do you know they held him in the trough before throwing him into the well?' the man asked with a suspicious glint in his eye.

Shit, he was right! Montalbano had made a colossal mistake, confusing Fazio with the corpse in the well! He was completely fried, his head wasn't working any more.

'Just do as I said!' he said sternly.

The man replied that he would get on to it as soon as he was finished with the corpse.

Then Dr Pasquano arrived with the ambulance and

stretcher bearers and immediately began to complain. 'What are you thinking? That I'm going to go down into the well to examine the corpse? Just pull him out for me, for the love of God!'

'We have to wait for Prosecutor Tommaseo to get here.'

'For heaven's sake, he drives so slowly the snails pass him! Next time don't call me until he's already here!'

It wasn't true. Prosecutor Tommaseo did not go so slowly that the snails passed him. The reality, known to one and all, was that he drove like a drunk dog. And, in fact, when he arrived on the scene, he said that it had taken him three hours to get there from Montelusa because he'd run off the road twice and a third time had crashed into a tree. He added that in running into the tree, he'd hit his forehead and therefore felt a little confused.

'Is it a man or a woman?' he asked the fire chief.

'Man.'

Immediately Tommaseo lost all interest in the case. All he cared about were corpses of the female variety, preferably naked, and crimes of passion.

'OK, OK. Pull him up. Good day.'

And he turned his back, got into his car, and drove off. Probably towards another tree. Everyone present, without exception, wished him Godspeed to you-know-where.

This time they added a second sling to the winch, a large piece of oilcloth with many ropes hanging from its sides. Montalbano felt sorry for the fireman, whose work was not going to be easy or pleasant. It was a job for a grave-digger. And as he was thinking this, the cars, the men, and the landscape started spinning all around him. He lost his balance, and to avoid falling to the ground like an empty sack, he grabbed Mimì's arm.

'Salvo, go home. I'll stay and take care of things. You should see your face,' said Mimì.

'No.'

'You can't even stand up!' Zito cut in. 'Do me a favour and go sit in the car at least.'

'No.' If he sat down, he would be out like a light in seconds.

At last, after many attempts and failures, the corpse appeared at the top of the well, wrapped like a mummy in the oilcloth and bound by the ropes, and was set down on the ground and untied.

Everybody drew near to look, covering their noses and mouths with their handkerchiefs. From what they could tell, it was a man just under sixty years old, completely naked, and in a rather bad state. His face was a pulp of flesh and bone. The fireman went back down into the well.

'What are you doing?'

'I want to get the blanket that was under the body.'

Pasquano, meanwhile, had a quick look at the dead man. 'I can't do anything here,' he said. 'Bring it to the lab for me.'

'How did he die, Doctor?'

'What's wrong with you, Montalbano? Has old age made you blind? Can't you see they emptied at least an entire magazine into his face?'

The Free Channel team arrived just in the nick of time to film the scene.

When they had finished, Zito approached Montalbano, gave him a big hug, and left with his colleagues.

*

As the Forensics team was leaving, Mallia the fire chief came up to the inspector.

'It might have been better for them to stay.'

'Why?'

'Because if we're unlucky enough to find some remains in the last well, we'll have to call them all back.'

'What a tragedy! Listen, please don't waste any time.'

Mallia gave an order, and the truck started towards the third well.

'Get in the car,' Mimì said to him.

'No, I'll walk.'

They didn't seem to realize that if he sat down, he was finished.

When he got to the well, he was drenched in sweat.

Lighting a cigarette, he noticed that his hand was trembling. There was nothing to be done about it.

What was keeping him on his feet was his anticipation of the fireman's response after he went down into the well.

How much fucking longer until they strapped him in?

'Can't they move a little faster?' he said in frustration.

'Calm down, Salvo. They're moving as fast as they can.'

At last they began to lower the fireman into the hole.

Matre santa, how slowly they were doing it! Just taking their merry old time! What, were they doing it just to drive him crazy? He couldn't stand waiting any longer. Taking a few steps back, he bent down, picked up a stone and threw it against a piece of scrap iron.

He missed by a good ten feet. He threw another stone and missed again. And again and again . . . After an eternity, he could tell by the sound of the crane that the fireman was coming back to the surface.

But when he got to the rim of the well, he didn't come all the way out. Only his head was visible. The fire chief drew near and whispered something in his ear. What the hell was this? And at that moment the inspector intercepted a glance between the fire chief and Mimì Augello. It was a matter of a split second, the batting of an eyelash. But enough for him to understand the meaning of it, as though the two had actually spoken.

'You've found him! He's in the well!'

He leapt forward, but was blocked by Mimì, who grabbed him and held on tight. Gallo, Galluzzo, and Lamarca, as if by prior arrangement, encircled them.

'Come on, Salvo, stop this nonsense,' said Mimì. 'Just calm down, for Christ's sake!'

'Anyway, Chief, we don't know yet whose body that is,' Gallo interjected.

'Lamarca, do me a favour and call them all back here: Forensics, the prosecutor, the—' Augello began.

'No!'

Montalbano shouted so loudly that even the firemen turned around.

'I'll tell you when to call them. Got that?' he said, shoving Augello aside.

Everybody looked at him in bewilderment. Suddenly he no longer felt tired. Now he was standing firm and steady, hands no longer trembling.

'But why not? We'll all save time that way,' said Augello.

'I don't want any outsiders to see him, all right? I don't want it! We'll weep over him first ourselves, and then we can call the others.'

SIX

Walking with a decisive step, Montalbano went right up to the edge of the well so that he would be the first to see. Dead silence fell over the scene, so dense that it weighed tons. The noise of the crane was like a drill.

The inspector bent his whole body forward, rose again, turned towards his men, and said: 'It's not him.'

Then his legs gave way, and he dropped slowly to his knees. Augello was quick to catch him before he fell on his face.

Montalbano then confusedly saw someone seize hold of him and put him in the squad car. He saw them lay him down on the back seat. And this was the last thing he saw, because he fell asleep at once, or lost consciousness, he couldn't tell which. Gallo left like a shot.

*

After he didn't know how long, he was woken up by a sudden braking that spilled him onto the floor of the car.

He cursed the saints. Then he heard Gallo's voice, also cursing.

'Fucking dog!'

To his surprise, he realized he felt rested. As if he'd had a whole night's sleep.

'How long have we been driving?'

'About an hour, Chief.'

'So we're near Montereale?'

'That's right, Chief.'

'Have we passed the Bar Reale?'

'We're just coming to it.'

'Good. Stop there.'

'But, Chief, you need to rest and—'

'Stop at the bar. I've had my rest, don't you worry.'

He downed two coffees, gave himself a thorough wash in the gents, then returned to the car.

'Let's go back.'

'But, Chief...'

'No arguments. Ring Augello's mobile and find out where things stand.'

After talking, Gallo gave him a report.

'Forensics are still at the scene, but they're almost finished. Tommaseo and Pasquano have already left.'

'All right. Tell Augello to wait for us at the drinking trough.'

*

'Forensics found two empty cartridge cases,' was the first thing Mimì said to him.

'Where?'

'Right beside the well. Nobody saw them earlier because they were hidden by all the firemen's equipment.'

'So Forensics has them?'

'Yes. But I was able to have a look at them and compare them with the one in my pocket that I found at the slipway. At a glance, they look the same to me.'

'Who was the dead man?'

'He had no papers on him. No name, about thirty.'

'How'd he die?'

'He fell.'

'What do you mean?'

'Just what I said. He died falling into the well. The damn thing's a hundred feet deep, for crying out loud.'

'When did he die?'

'About ten hours ago, max, according to Pasquano.'

'Are we sure there were no gunshot wounds on the body?'

'Pretty sure.'

'Then let's not waste any more time.'

'Tell us what you want us to do.'

'I've changed my mind. Let's wait a little longer before informing the commissioner. First let's have a look around ourselves.'

'Yes, I agree. But do you have any sense of what might have happened?'

'Look, everyone, what I think happened is this: at some point Fazio, realizing they were going to throw him into the well, must have reacted wildly, so that one of the thugs holding him prisoner ended up falling into the well instead of him. And then he ran away, but the other one started shooting, forcing him to stop.'

'But if that's how it went, then why, once he caught Fazio again, didn't he just shoot him and throw him into the well as they'd planned to do from the start?'

'That's a good point. But the fact is that he's not in the well. So we have to look for him elsewhere, but still in the general vicinity.'

'Where should we start?'

'Over by Monte Scibetta. See that little house down there, near the electricity pylon? Go there in the car, search the house, and if you don't find anything in it, take the little track behind it – it's the only one there – and drive up to the top. The mountain is full of caves and crags. Call his name from time to time. Maybe he can't move. We'll stay in touch with each other via mobile phone.'

'All right. And what about you?'

'I've got a little idea of my own. We'll talk again in an hour.'

*

'Where are you going?' asked Gallo.

'Into the tunnel that runs through the mountain.'

'I think I heard that you can't go in. It's closed.'

'Let's have a look anyway.'

The tunnel entrance was sealed by a palisade of dank, rotten planks. Cars, of course, could not pass through, but people could.

In fact, to the right, two planks had been smashed, making it possible to walk straight in. Apparently the tunnel served as a nocturnal shelter for vagabonds, or as a safe place for taking drugs.

'We have to go in with the car,' said Montalbano.

'Why?'

'It's pitch black in there. We need the headlights.'

'I'll go and have a look,' said Gallo, getting out of the car.

The inspector watched him go up to the palisade. Gallo took a step back, raised his right leg, and dealt a forceful kick to one of the planks. It gave way like tissue paper.

'Get out of the car,' Gallo said to the inspector, getting back into the driver's seat.

Montalbano obeyed. Gallo started it, approached the barrier ever so slowly, and when the bumper touched the wood, he continued forward, applying more and more pressure. After a moment, half the palisade fell away, creating an opening a truck could have passed through.

Montalbano returned to the car and got in. The headlights lit the tunnel. Suddenly, to the right, they noticed what looked like a man lying down. They got a better look. It was a pile of clothes and blankets riddled with holes.

Bothered by the light, a cat dashed out from under the rags and ran away.

'That cat doesn't have it so bad,' said Montalbano, 'with all the mice there must be in here.'

'Chief, that wasn't a cat, but a rat,' said Gallo. 'We'll have to be careful if we get out of the car. They might eat us alive.'

They'd gone another fifty yards or so when a shot suddenly struck the windscreen square in the middle.

They leapt out of the car at the same time, Montalbano to the right and Gallo to the left, and sprawled on the ground. Then, after a brief pause, Gallo started sliding backwards and, leaning on his elbows, passed behind the car and around, until he was beside the inspector.

'Are you hurt?'

'No. You?'

'Me neither.'

They spoke softly, into each other's ear. The car's engine was still running, the headlights still on, lighting up a long stretch of tunnel. But there wasn't a soul to be seen. Where had the shot come from?

'You armed, Chief?' asked Gallo.

'No.'

'I am.'

'If he's clever, he should shoot out the headlights. Why doesn't he?'

'Maybe because he doesn't want us to know where he is, or because he hasn't got many bullets left.'

'Look. I think I see a sort of white streak along the wall, over there on the right – it sort of zigzags and then stops, about ten yards ahead.'

'You're right. It must be a recess in the tunnel wall, a kind of lay-by.'

'Then he's there.'

'Who?'

'Whoever's holding Fazio. He must have recognized the police car.'

'What should we do?'

'We have to do something immediately. I'm afraid he's going to get some brilliant idea.'

'What can he do?'

'Well, if he comes out in the open holding a gun to Fazio's head, all we can do is stand aside and let him leave, probably in our car!'

'And so?'

'Listen. Let's get back in the car, really quietly, without closing the doors. Then we'll reverse slowly.'

'OK.'

'Stay as low as you can, because once he hears us leaving, he's going to start shooting again.' They moved very carefully, climbed into the car, expecting at any moment to be shot at. But nothing happened. The windscreen had a round hole in it, with a spider's web of cracks all around it. But they could still see through it OK.

'What should I do now?' Gallo asked when, still in reverse, they were almost at the tunnel entrance.

'All right, listen closely. Now we're going to go forward at high speed with the siren on, and—'

'Why the siren?'

'Because it should make a tremendous noise in here, which will confuse him. When we reach the recess in the wall, you're going to brake and swerve so that it will be lit up by the headlights. Give me your gun.'

Gallo handed it to him. Montalbano braced himself with one hand clutching the dashboard from underneath, then leaned out of the open door with three-quarters of his body, pointing the weapon forward, ready to shoot.

'Now be sure to make the car turn so that it lights up the recess. I can't do anything until I know exactly where Fazio is. I don't want to shoot him by accident.'

'No problem, Chief.'

'Go!'

Gallo outdid himself. The moment he reached the recess, the front of the car spun to the right, as if it wanted to enter it, and suddenly stopped. In the layby they saw a man dazzled by the headlights and disorientated by the siren, sticking his arm out and firing one shot blindly, left forearm covering his eyes. He had no time to do anything else. Already out of the car before it had stopped, Montalbano dealt him a swift kick in the stomach. The man fell to the ground, writhing in pain, and let go of his pistol. Montalbano bent down to look at him. He paled. It wasn't Fazio's captor. It was Fazio.

*

It was more than obvious that he hadn't recognized them and still didn't recognize them. The wound to his head wasn't deep, but must have been severe enough to make him lose his memory. As they were putting him in the car, he tried to escape, swinging at Montalbano's face, though the inspector miraculously managed to dodge the punch.

'Handcuff him.'

'Handcuff Fazio?!'

'Don't be an idiot, Gallo. Don't you see he can't tell his friends from his enemies? He must have a pretty high fever.'

'Should we take him to the hospital?'

'Of course. And in a hurry. We'll go to Fiacca.'

'Why not Montelusa?'

'It's better if everyone thinks we haven't found him yet. And it's even better if they don't know which hospital he's in. Let's go now, and give me your mobile.'

The first call was to Mimì. He explained what had happened and told him to go back to Vigàta. The second was to Fazio's wife.

But before dialling, he turned to Fazio. 'Want to talk to your wife?'

Fazio acted as if he hadn't heard and merely stared into the space in front of him. So the inspector phoned her and told her the whole story.

'How is he?' was the only thing she wanted to know.

'He's got a wound to the head, but it doesn't look too serious to me. He's lost his memory. I'll call you as soon as we get him to a hospital. But please don't worry, it's going to be all right.'

If only all women were like that! he thought, turning the phone off. For the whole drive, Fazio didn't open his mouth. He didn't even look out of the window. He kept his eyes glued to the back of Gallo's head, as they raced wildly through the barren landscape.

*

Some two hours later, they were back on the road to Montelusa. In the opinion of the doctor who examined him, Fazio was suffering from cranial trauma. The wound itself was minor. The memory loss could have been caused by two things: shock or something involving the brain. But the doctor couldn't tell them much for another twenty-four hours. At any rate, it didn't seem like anything life-threatening. Montalbano informed the wife, who said she would leave at once for Fiacca.

'Would you like me to send a car to take you there?'

'No, thank you, there's no need.'

*

Now that everything had been resolved, fatigue started to crash down on him, bit by bit, so that by the time he got home to Marinella, he barely had time to open the front door and close it before he fell to his knees like a horse that can't take another step.

There wasn't a muscle in his body that wasn't slack.

He crawled on all fours to the bedroom, climbed onto the bed, still fully dressed, gripping the covers, and fell immediately into a fathomless sleep.

*

He woke up the following morning around eight. He'd slept for twelve hours straight and felt completely rested, but was so hungry that he could have eaten the legs of a chair. How long had it been since he'd had a proper meal? He went to the fridge, opened it, and felt heartsick. Empty, as desolate as a desert. Not even an olive, a sardine, a piece of tumazzo. But how was it that Adelina hadn't ... But Adelina ... Adel ...

All at once he remembered.

And at the same moment, he wished he had lost his memory like Fazio. They say the light of truth makes him upon whom it shines rejoice and keeps him warm. Whereas the light of the truth that shone on Montalbano – which in this case was the little light inside the fridge – froze him, turned him instantly into a block of ice.

He'd completely forgotten about Livia, Jesus fucking Christ!

He called her name, not moving, since he was unable to take so much as a single step.

'Livia!'

The voice that came out of his mouth sounded rather like a cat mewling. No, Livia was nowhere around, there was no point in calling her name. With great effort he unfroze, went back into the bedroom, and looked around. No trace of Livia whatsoever, as though she'd never come down from Boccadasse. He went into the dining room.

On the table was a letter.

A last goodbye, no doubt. For good, this time, with no change of mind possible. How could he blame her? All the same, he didn't have the courage to pick it up just yet. Before reading it, he needed to pull himself together, to find the strength necessary to listen to what he deserved to hear. He took all his clothes off, threw them into the laundry basket, showered and shaved, made some coffee, drank three cups one after the other, got dressed, phoned the hospital, and managed to talk to Mrs Fazio.

'Any news?'

'They have to operate on him, Inspector.'

'Why?'

'He has a cerebral haematoma.'

'Due to the wound?'

'The doctor says he must have fallen and hit his head in the same place as the wound.'

'When is the operation?'

'I don't know. Sometime this morning, in any case.'

'I'll be right over.'

'Listen, Inspector, the chief physician here, who's a wonderful person, told me his life is not in danger, and it's a relatively easy operation. But just in case, take down my mobile number.'

'Thanks, I'll take it down, but I'm coming anyway.' He hung up, took Livia's letter, and went out on the veranda and sat down.

Dearest Salvo,

After waiting for you for three hours (we had agreed we were going to have dinner together, remember?) I got absolutely furious.

As I was about to ring you, I had an idea: to come to the police station in person and start slapping you in front of everyone. I wanted to make an ugly scene that your men would remember for a long time.

So I called a taxi and came to the station. I told Catarella I wanted to see you and he replied that you weren't in your office. When I asked him if he knew what time you'd be back, he said he didn't know. And he added that the only thing he knew was that you'd had to go to Montelusa.

Since I had no intention of abandoning my plan to slap you, I told him I would wait for you in your room. Which I did.

But a few minutes later Catarella appeared.

He closed the door behind him, started acting mysterious, and

ANDREA CAMILLERI

said he wanted to talk to me, even though he wasn't convinced he was doing the right thing. And he told me that in his opinion, something had happened to Fazio.

Something serious, because you had seemed very concerned.

That was when I understood in a flash that if you'd totally forgotten about your appointment with me, then the situation must be very dire.

I know how much you care about Fazio.

And so my anger simmered down immediately.

I went to have a bite to eat at Enzo's and then got in another taxi and went back to Marinella. Around 6 p.m., I phoned Catarella. He told me there was no news, and that you weren't back yet.

And so I thought that if I stayed around I might just get in the way.

I reserved a seat on the ten o'clock flight for tomorrow morning. I sincerely hope everything turns out all right.

So, too bad for now. Maybe next time.

There's only one thing I hold against you: not having found the time to call me and tell me what was happening.

Please keep me informed about Fazio.

A big hug,

Forever yours

    Livia

It would have been a thousand times better if Livia had written a letter full of obscenities, insults, and abuse. This way, it only made him feel like the shit that he was.

Or maybe Livia had written him so understanding a letter just to humiliate him all the more. Because, even admitting that his tremendous concern for Fazio had muddled his brain, there still was no excuse for not having even given Livia a ring. How on earth had she managed to slip his mind entirely?

'*It's not just absurd,*' said Montalbano Two. '*The truth is that you erased Livia completely from your consciousness. That was why you didn't phone her. Because there was nobody left in your head to phone.*'

'*And what are you getting at with that observation?*' Montalbano One asked polemically.

'*I'm not getting at anything. I'm simply saying that Livia is only intermittently present in your thoughts.*'

'*OK, fine, but now that Livia is in fact extremely present in my thoughts for the moment, what, in your opinion, should I do?*'

'*Call her at once.*'

Instead Montalbano decided not to call her.

At that hour she was already at the office, and the phone call would have necessarily been short and constrained. No, he would call her that evening, when he would have all the time he needed to sort things out. The best thing to do right now was to leave at once for Fiacca.

But before getting in his car, he rang Fazio's wife.

'He's in theatre, Inspector. There's no point coming now. They won't even let me see him.'

'Could you call the station after the operation and let us know how it went? I would be very grateful.'

SEVEN

The moment he saw the inspector, Catarella nearly threw himself at his feet.

'Jeezis, Chief, I ain't seen yiz f'such a long time! I rilly rilly missed yiz! An' Gallo tol' me ivryting! Ann' 'iss mornin' I call a haspitol an' Fazio's wife tol' me 'at—'

'Everything's fine, Cat. And thanks.'

'Fer what, Chief?'

'For talking to Livia.'

Catarella turned fire-red.

'Ah, y'gotta 'scuze me, Chief, f'takin' a libbity, but the young lady, insomuch as she lookt rilly upset, she—'

'You did exactly the right thing, Cat. Now send me Inspector Augello.'

*

'Any news of Fazio?' was Mimì's first question.

'He's under the knife.'

'Gallo told me he didn't recognize either of you.'

'He even shot at us! But he's going to recover, you'll see. What did Pasquano say about the second corpse?'

'He didn't find any bullet or knife wounds. The man was simply chucked into the well still alive. In my opinion, your hypothesis that it was Fazio who pushed him in self-defence is probably correct.'

'Has he been identified?'

'Not yet. He had no documents. Forensics took his fingerprints. But I don't think they'll find anything.'

'You think he's clean?'

'No, but I saw his hands.'

'What do you mean?'

'As he was falling, he must have tried desperately to grab hold of something, without success. He didn't have any fingertips left, all the flesh was scraped off.'

'We'll know more when Fazio can talk again. And what can you tell me about the other corpse?'

'The first one we found? I'm still waiting to hear from Forensics.'

'And have you spoken to Pasquano?'

'Nobody can talk to him! If I try it'll turn into a shouting match.'

'I'll call him myself, but not till later in the morning.'

'Listen, don't get pissed off, but . . .'

'But what?'

'Don't you think it's time to inform Bonetti-Alderighi about what happened to Fazio?'

'Why do you say that?'

'I wouldn't want him to find out from somebody else.'

'From whom?'

'I dunno, maybe some journalist.'

'Zito doesn't talk.'

'Zito's not in question. But just think about it, Salvo. Fazio's at Fiacca Hospital, under his own first and last name, for a head wound caused by a firearm. Now, imagine some journalist from Fiacca—'

'You're right.'

'And bear in mind that you'll have to grant Fazio convalescent leave. What are you going to tell the commissioner, that he had typhoid fever?'

'You're right.'

'I wouldn't waste any more time, if I were you.'

'I'll do it right now.'

He dialled the direct number to the commissioner's office and turned on the speakerphone as soon as he heard someone pick up.

'Hello, Montalbano here. I'd like to—'

'Dear Montalbano, how are you? And the family?'

It was that colossal pain in the arse Dr Lattes, chief of the commissioner's cabinet, who held the unshakable belief that the inspector was married and had a large family.

'Everybody's fine, with thanks to the Blessed Virgin.'

'We must always give thanks. Did you wish to speak with the commissioner?'

'Yes.'

'Unfortunately he had to go to Palermo and won't be

back until late afternoon tomorrow. If you'd like to tell me—'

'I wanted to inform the commissioner that one of my men was wounded in a firefight, and therefore—'

'Is it serious?'

'No.'

'Thank God!'

We must always give thanks! Will you let him know?'

'Of course! And please give my very best wishes to the family.'

'I certainly will.'

Mimì, who'd listened to the exchange, stared at the inspector, wonderstruck.

'What's the matter with you?' asked Montalbano.

'But ... are you married with children?'

'Don't be stupid, Mimì.'

'So then why, with Lattes ...'

'I'll explain later, all right? Actually, no, you know what I say? I say that since we've got nothing to go on yet, you're going to go back to your office now, and I'm going to sign a few stacks of papers.'

*

Two hours later, with his right arm stiff from too many signatures, he decided it was time to call Dr Pasquano. But as he picked up the receiver, he realized that if the doctor's balls were in a spin, as they often were, then he was liable to tell the inspector to get stuffed and say nothing about the corpses. The best thing, therefore, was to go and talk to him in person. Before leaving the office, however, he rang Adelina and told her that Livia had left, and that the coast was therefore clear.

'I c'n imagine a candition the good woman a lefta house in,' said Adelina, who never forgave Livia anything.

'What condition do you think, Adelì? It's clean!'

''Assa whatta you say, cuzza you's a man anna you don'a notice a nuttin'! She always a leave it uppa side down! You know where I fine a pair odda younga lady's socks one time? Jess guess!'

'C'mon, Adelì, this isn't a quiz show.'

'I tink I canna mebbe come dis aftanoon. You wann' I make a somethin' a eat a fer tonite?'

'That would be wonderful.'

The moment he hung up, the phone rang again. It was Fazio's wife.

'Everything's fine, Inspector. The operation is over, and it went very well. They told me I can see him around five o'clock. But the doctors don't want any other visitors. So it'd be better if you came tomorrow morning.'

'All right. But if you'd like to go home and rest for a little while, I could send one of my—'

'Thank you, Inspector, but don't worry, my sister's here with me.'

As he passed Catarella's post on his way out of the office, he informed him: 'Mrs Fazio just called. The operation was a complete success. Tell everyone.'

As he was parking in front of the Institute, he saw Dr Pasquano standing outside the main entrance, smoking a cigarette.

'Good morning, Doctor.'

'If you say so.'

Always so cordial, the good doctor. But he seemed only half angry, since he didn't start insulting the inspector.

'I didn't know you had the vice,' Montalbano said, just to make conversation.

'What vice are you referring to?'

'Smoking.'

'Never had that one.'

'But you're smoking!'

'Montalbano, you think just like a cop, which is no surprise.'

'And how do I think?'

'You link a man with a single act, whereas that man is not always engaged in that act . . .'

'What are you doing, Doctor? Misquoting Pirandello? You know what I say to you?'

'Do tell.'

'That I don't give a flying fuck whether you have the vice or not.'

'That's a little better, though you've still come to annoy me and ruin the only cigarette I'll smoke all day.'

'Even one cigarette a day is a vice, according to the Americans.'

'You can all go fuck yourselves, you and the Americans.'

'Keep your voice down, or President Bush will have you bombed at once. Anything new to tell me?'

'Who, me?! How could I have anything new to tell you? By now I've seen every manner of violent death imaginable. All I'm missing, to round out my collection, is death by napalm.'

'I meant anything new about the two bodies found in the wells.'

'I worked that out perfectly well all by myself. I was hardly under the delusion that you'd come to ask after my health.'

'Let me remedy that at once: how are you?'

'At the moment I can't complain. And thank you for your courteous, ready interest. Where shall we start?'

'With the second one, the younger body.'

'You mean the fresher one? He died when somebody threw him into the well. He was fine before that.'

'Did he have any marks of a struggle?'

'Can't you see you're getting soft in the head with age? A man falls a hundred feet into a well, bouncing between the walls all the way down, and you're asking me if . . . Come on! You want some advice?'

'If you must.'

'Given your age, why don't you just pack up and resign? Can't you see for yourself that you're not right in the head any more? Both heads, actually, above and below.'

'Doctor, I think you're laying it on a little thick.'

'I'm a physician. We're supposed to tell the truth, always.'

'And do you? Even when you're bluffing at poker?'

'When I'm playing poker, I'm not a doctor, but a poker player. But as for you, didn't you see the body?'

'No, Doctor, I had to leave shortly before they pulled it out of the well.'

It was half lie, half truth. Apparently Augello hadn't told him that Montalbano had passed out. Otherwise one could only imagine what Pasquano would have said.

'About thirty years old, in good health, good shape, a perfect recruit for the lists of hell. He would have lived to be a hundred, if not for shoot-outs and a variety of potential accidents.'

'And the other?'

'The other one . . . Shall we go into my surgery?'

They went inside, entered Pasquano's room, and the doctor told him to sit down.

'How long had he been in the well?' the inspector began.

'For at least a week. Which accelerated the decomposition. They must have thrown him in shortly after killing him. But I also have to tell you — and this is only an opinion, mind you — that they took a little while to finish him off. Let's say a good half day.'

'You mean they tortured him?'

'Well, I wouldn't know . . . but . . .'

'Doctor, you were much more decisive in your younger days. Now you've even got a tremor in your voice. You want some advice? Why don't you retire to the private life so you can play poker all day from morning till night? I'm only trying to help, since it pains me a little to see you this way. I promise you that whatever you tell me, even if it's totally fucking stupid, won't leave this room.'

Pasquano started laughing.

'You really can't take it, can you? Well, all right. Bear in mind that what I'm about to tell you won't be written in my report. In my opinion, the first thing they did to him was shoot him in the foot.'

'Which one?'

'What difference does it make? The left.'

'Evidently they wanted to make him talk.'

'Maybe. They left him that way for a few hours, then worked him over with a knife — he had cuts all over his body — and then they stabbed him five times to kill him. Three times in the chest and twice in the face.'

'So he's unrecognizable.'

'These idiotic comments of yours drive me insane! Didn't you see for yourself the state he'd been reduced to?!'

'Were you able to tell whether he was dressed when—'

'He was already naked; he wasn't stripped afterwards.'

'And when they shot him in the foot, was it already bare too?'

'A strangely intelligent question, coming from you.

Yes, it was already bare. They surprised him in his sleep, naked. And after killing him, they wrapped him in a blanket that was there at hand.'

Montalbano remained silent.

'Mind telling me what thought is taxing your poor brain?' Pasquano asked.

'I'm thinking that to make someone talk, normally you don't shoot him in the foot. You burn his hand, you gouge out an eye . . . All the little knife cuts may make sense, but shooting his foot . . .'

'They were very well taken care of.'

'Who were?'

'The feet.'

'Spent a lot of time at the chiropodist's?'

'I'd say so.'

'Notice anything else?'

'He'd been operated on, a long time ago, on his right leg. An excellent job, I must say.'

'What for?'

'A torn ligament.'

'So he limped?'

'Not necessarily.'

'Got anything else to tell me?'

'Yes.'

'Tell me.'

'Get the hell out of here.'

*

Driving back to Vigàta, he noticed he was going 100 kilo-metres an hour, something he never did. He slowed down, realizing that what was pressing his foot onto the accel-erator was the violent hunger that had come over him as he left the Institute. He entered the trattoria in such a rush that Enzo, seeing him race in, asked: 'Something happen?'

'No, nothing.'

Montalbano sat down at his usual table.

'What can I get you?'

'Everything.'

He stuffed himself shamefully. It was a good thing there weren't any other patrons there, aside from a man who never looked away from the newspaper propped against a bottle in front of him.

When Montalbano had finished, Enzo congratulated him.

'Enjoy it in good health, Inspector.'

'Thanks.'

'Would you like a *digestivo*?'

'No.'

There wasn't room for even a drop of water in his belly. If he had a digestive, he would explode like the fat man in the Monty Python movie.

When he got into the car, it actually seemed smaller. Walking along the jetty, he took very small steps, perhaps because he couldn't walk any faster, perhaps just to make it last longer. When he got to the flat rock, he sat down.

Despite his long sleep the night before, he suddenly felt very woozy. Apparently he still hadn't caught up. He turned back, got into the car, and headed off to Marinella to sleep for a couple of hours.

*

He reappeared at the station just before five o'clock.

'Ahh, Chief, Chief! Seein' as how F'rinsix sint a f'rinsic pitcher o' one o' the two disseasts inna well, I soitched a soitch o' poissons whereforwhom'z reported as missing.'

'And?'

'Nuttin', Chief, zwaz nuttin'.'

'And did they tell you anything about the other one?'

'Nuttin', Chief.'

'Try and see if there's anything among last week's reports about a man around sixty who'd had an operation on his right leg.'

'Straightaways, Chief.'

'In the meantime, send me Fazio.'

Catarella, amazed, stared at him.

'Sorry, I meant Galluzzo.'

The habit was so ingrained . . . A sudden twinge of melancholy pricked him, unexpectedly.

'Your orders, Chief.'

*

Mrs Fazio phoned around six.

'They let me see him! And he recognized me straight-away! The first thing he said was that he wanted to see

103

the chief. So I went and asked for the chief of surgery, who was still at the hospital. When he came into the room, my husband got angry. It was you he wanted to see!'

'Did you tell him I'm coming to see him tomorrow morning?'

'Yes, Inspector.'

*

What with one thing and the other, it was suddenly eight o'clock. Montalbano decided it was time to leave. Not that he was hungry, at lunch he'd eaten tons, he was just tired of being in the office.

Passing Catarella, he said goodbye and he was just about to get in the car when out of the corner of his eye he saw Catarella come flying out of the building towards him like a ball from a cannon.

'What's wrong?'

'Ahh, Chief, Chief! Iss the c'mishner's onna tiliphone. Jeezus, Chief, y'oughter 'ear 'is voice, y'oughter!'

'Why, what kind of voice has he got?'

''Slike a lion inna jangle!'

EIGHT

Cursing the saints, he went back into his office, and the moment he said 'Hello' into the receiver, he was assailed by an enraged commissioner.

'You are completely out of your mind! This is insane! Stuff for the madhouse!'

'But weren't they abolished?'

It had slipped out. Luckily Mr C'mishner didn't even hear it.

'There's a firefight, one of our men is wounded – thank God not seriously – and with a little phone call to Lattes, you wipe your hands of it! Utter insanity!'

'Who else was I supposed to call, since you weren't there?'

'All right, but you should at least have left a detailed report on my desk! Come here at once. I'll be waiting for you.'

There was no way he could go. Because if he was

asked exactly how Fazio was wounded, he wouldn't know what the hell to reply.

'Just right now I can't, Mr Commissioner.'

'Listen, Montalbano, I am ordering you—'

'I just got a call from the hospital telling me that Fazio, my man, has regained consciousness and wants to see me . . .'

'Then come to my office immediately after you see him.'

'But the hospital's in Fiacca!'

'Wait a second! Fiacca is not in your jurisdiction! Why did you take him there?'

'Because we found Fazio not far from the outskirts of—'

'Found? What do you mean, "found"?'

'Mr Commissioner, sir, it's a very complicated story.'

'Then you can explain it all to me tomorrow morning at nine o'clock sharp.'

Jesus, what a pain in the arse! He had to come up with another lie, quick.

'I'm terribly sorry, sir, but I can't make it at nine.'

'You're joking, aren't you?'

Montalbano lowered his voice and assumed a conspiratorial tone.

'It's a very private matter, you see, and I wouldn't want anyone—'

'Postpone it!'

'I can't, sir, believe me, I really can't! You see, Dr Gruntz is coming all the way from Zurich.'

'And who is this doctor?'

'He's the top specialist in the field.'

'What field?'

That, indeed, was the question. In what damn field might a Swiss named Gruntz be the top specialist? Better glide over it. Muddy the waters a little more. He didn't answer the question directly.

'He's coming straight to my house at nine thirty, to perform a double Scrockson on me, the effects of which — as I'm sure you know — can last from three up to five hours. And so I'll have to lie still in bed for that time. But I could definitely come to see you in the afternoon.'

'I'm sorry, but what did you say Dr Gruntz is coming to do?' the commissioner asked, apparently impressed.

'The double Scrockson.'

'And what's its purpose?'

What indeed could be the purpose of something with such a highfalutin name? Montalbano blurted out the first whopper that came into his head.

'What, you mean you don't know? It's a Western adaptation of a procedure practised by Indian yogis. It involves inserting a plastic tube into the anus, which is then expertly, painstakingly manoeuvred so that it comes out of—'

'That's quite enough, thank you! I'll expect you tomorrow afternoon at four o'clock.'

*

When he got home to Marinella, the only sun left was a reddish strip of sky on the sea horizon. The surf was panting softly. No sign of any birds. His conversation with the commissioner had whetted an appetite that hadn't existed before he picked up the phone. Maybe it was the desire for a kind of compensation. He'd once read that in antiquity, after a plague had ended, people would eat and fuck like there was no tomorrow. But could he really liken Bonetti-Alderighi to a plague? Well, maybe not the plague, but cholera, yes, sort of.

Opening the fridge, he felt as if he was looking at a great discovery, some sort of vast treasure piled up by brigands. Adelina had gone overboard cooking for him. The works: aubergine Parmigiana, pasta with sausage, caponata, aubergine dumplings, *caciocavallo di Ragusa*, and passuluna olives. Apparently there wasn't any fresh fish at the market. He laid the table on the veranda, and as the aubergine Parmigiana and pasta were warming up, he drank two glasses of cold white wine to Fazio's health. When he got up to phone Livia, a good three hours had passed.

He slept badly.

*

As he was about to leave for Fiacca, at eight thirty the following morning, it occurred to him that at his normal cruising speed, as Livia so irritatingly called it, by the time he got to the hospital, Fazio was liable to be already discharged. So he called the police station.

'Ahh, what izzit, Chief? Ahh? Wha' happened?' asked Catarella, immediately alarmed.

'Nothing's happened, Cat. Calm down. I just want you to tell Gallo to come and pick me up in Marinella and take me to Fiacca.'

'Straightaways, Chief.'

But the truth of the matter was that he just didn't feel like driving. He was too agitated. His curiosity to know what Fazio had to tell him was eating him alive. It had come over him the moment he'd lain down in bed and hadn't left him since. Indeed he'd spent practically the whole night forming hypotheses and conjectures, all without the slightest foundation.

About ten minutes later he heard the siren of the squad car approaching at high speed. Imagine Gallo missing a chance to race around with the siren on!

He always watched Gallo closely when sitting beside him during drives when they had to get somewhere fast. Gallo at the wheel seemed loose and relaxed; he was an excellent driver, and clearly it gave him a great deal of pleasure. Sometimes, perhaps without realizing it, he would start murmuring the words to a little children's song: *La beddra Betta / cu 'na quasetta* ... And so Montalbano realized that when at the wheel of a wildly speeding car, Gallo lost at least thirty years and became a little kid again.

'Did you have a pedal car when you were little?' the inspector asked him as they were leaving for Fiacca.

Gallo gave him a confused look.

'Why do you ask?'

'I dunno, just making conversation.'

'No, sir, I never did. I always wanted one, but my father could never afford to buy me one.'

Maybe that was why . . . But then he suddenly felt embarrassed at the thought that had come into his head. Which was that Gallo's passion for driving fast was a compensation for what he'd missed as a child. American-movie stuff, like when they tell you that someone became a rapist because his father had abused him when he was little.

In his younger days, such thoughts would never even have grazed the surface of his brain. Apparently with age, even the brain slackens, like the muscles and skin . . . His eye fell on the speedometer: 170.

'Don't you think you're going a little fast?'

'Want me to slow down?'

He was about to say yes, but he wanted to get there and talk to Fazio as soon as possible.

'No, but be careful. I don't want to end up in a body cast in the bed next to Fazio's.'

*

The inspector was in the habit of getting lost in hospitals. And to think that he did everything possible to avoid the problem. Not only would he get precise instructions upon entering as to which lift to take, which floor to get off at, which ward to visit, but . . . It was hopeless. In the brief distance travelled between the information desk and the lift area, he would completely forget everything he'd been told. And so, once inside lift A instead of lift B, he would inevitably end up in the neurosurgery ward when he was supposed to go to accident and emergency. And then began a veritable *via crucis* to find the right ward. He would go down the wrong corridors, open doors exposing naked patients, and have endless insults heaped upon him . . .

This time, too, the tradition was maintained. In short, after he'd been wandering the corridors for about half an hour, lost and covered in sweat, a nurse of about thirty, tall and blonde with blue-green eyes and long legs like one of those unreal nurses one sees in hospital dramas, crossed paths with him for the second time and, noticing he looked unhappier than ever, like an orphan from Burundi, took pity on him and asked:

'Excuse me, are you looking for someone?'

'Yes.'

'If you tell me where you want to go, I'll take you there.'

In his mind Montalbano prayed that the Good Lord, after granting her the title in the worldwide Miss Nurse contest, would throw open the pearly gates for her when she died. The young woman left him outside the door to Fazio's room, which was closed.

He knocked discreetly, but nobody answered. Already agitated, he broke out in a cold sweat. Maybe they'd changed his room?

So how was he going to work out where they'd moved him to? Perhaps it was best to have a look first, and see if the room was actually empty. As he was reaching for the handle like a burglar trying not to make a sound, the door was suddenly opened from the inside, and Fazio's wife appeared.

'Let's talk outside,' she whispered to him, closing the door behind her.

'What's wrong?' asked Montalbano, worried.

The woman had two dark circles under her eyes, and the inspector thought he saw more white hair on her head than the last time he'd seen her.

'I just wanted to let you know that my husband didn't have a good night. He had nightmares. The doctor said he shouldn't talk to you for more than five minutes. I'm so sorry, Inspector, but—'

'I understand perfectly, signora. Don't worry, I won't tire him out, I promise.'

At this point a dwarflike nurse materialized next to Fazio's wife and, without saying hello, cast a malevolent glance at the inspector and then looked at her watch.

'You have exactly five minutes, starting now.'

What was this, a race against the clock?

Mrs Fazio opened the door for him, then slowly closed it behind him. She understood that the inspector wanted to be alone when talking to her husband. What a great woman!

Fazio was either sleeping or keeping his eyes closed. The only part of his body not under the sheet was his head, which looked like a pilot's from the early days of aviation, when they wore a kind of leather cap that covered the neck and ears as well, leaving only the face uncovered. The only difference was that Fazio's was made of gauze.

To Montalbano it looked as if the part of his face that was visible between the cheekbones and mouth had changed, with the skin resting directly on the bone and no flesh in between. Maybe it was the effect of the bandaging. Beside the head of the bed was a metal chair, which Montalbano quietly sat down in. What to do now? Wake him up or let him sleep? His curiosity was strong, but he overcame it out of affection for Fazio. Even if the investigation was held up for a day, no harm would be done. At that moment, Fazio opened his eyes, looked at him, and recognized him.

'Chief . . .' he said in a weary, faraway voice that nevertheless had a note of happiness in it.

'Hi,' said Montalbano, touched.

And he took into his own the hand that Fazio had pulled out from under the sheet. They remained that way for a few moments, not saying anything, each enjoying the other's warmth. Then Fazio spoke.

'I still don't remember too well.'

'You can tell me everything when it all comes back to you. There's no hurry.'

But Fazio wasn't ready to give up.

'Someone I used to know started calling me on the phone . . . Used to be a ballet dancer when he was young . . . We went to primary school together . . .'

'What's his name?'

'I don't remember . . .'

A sort of flash went off in Montalbano's head. He hesitated a moment, then blurted out a name at random.

'Manzella?'

The inspector clearly saw Fazio give a start in surprise.

'Yes, sir! That's him! Damn, you are good, Chief!'

'And what did he want from you?'

Fazio closed his eyes. It was like a signal, because at that moment the door opened and the dwarf came in.

'Conversation's over.'

Not even in Sing-Sing could the guards be so severe.

'Are you sure your watch is right?' the inspector asked.

'Down to the split second. Out!'

He got up and started walking ever so slowly on purpose, just to anger the nurse. When he was in front of her, he asked: 'When can I come back?'

'Visitors are allowed every afternoon from four to seven.'

'And how much time will you give me?'

'Another five minutes.'

'Could we make that ten?'

'Seven.'

Oh, well, better than nothing.

Out in the corridor, leaning against the wall, was Mrs Fazio. 'Couldn't you ask them to give you a chair?'

'It's not allowed. But I'm going back in now. Did you manage to talk a little with him?'

'Yes, but not much. He seemed very weak.'

'The doctors say there's nothing to worry about, that he's getting better by the hour. When are you coming back?'

'This afternoon at four.'

When he reached the end of the corridor, he had a choice between right and left. He stopped, doubtful. Which direction had he come from? He thought he remembered arriving from the left. So he went down that corridor, which not only was endless, but every single door on the ward was closed. Halfway down, he saw a lift. Should he take it or not? He had no choice, since the architect who'd built the hospital had forgotten to put any staircases in it. The doors opened, he went in and immediately noticed that the panel of buttons was missing the letter G, for ground floor. There were only three numbers, in fact: 4, 5 and 6. It must have been a service lift that went only to those three floors. Meanwhile the door had closed again, and so he pressed button 5. His heart sank at the thought that he would have to struggle again before he found the way out. The lift stopped, the door opened, and before him stood the nurse who had shown him the way to Fazio's room. She must have understood right away that he was lost again, and Montalbano had to suppress the urge to embrace her.

'Tell me frankly: are you my guardian angel?' he asked her, stepping out of the lift.

'Certainly not, but I'll do my best to help anyway.'

'Would you show me to the exit?'

'The best I can do is to show you to the right lift.'

'Thank you. To whom do I have the pleasure of speaking, if I may?'

'Angela.'

'You see? I was right.'

'And you?'

'Salvo. Salvo Montalbano. I'm a police inspector.'

'Oh, great!'

'Why do you say that?'

'A police inspector getting lost inside a hospital?'

'It happens to me all the time. Listen, Angela, I have to come back this afternoon at four o'clock. Will you still be here?'

'Yes.'

'Could you do me a favour?'

'That depends.'

'Could you wait for me at the entrance?'

'Is this a date?'

'No, just a desperate cry for help.'

Angela started laughing, and didn't say yes or no.

*

'How's Fazio?' Gallo asked as the inspector was getting in the car.

'He's a little weak, but he's actually fine. We'll be coming back this afternoon at four, so I want you to be ready at the station by two thirty. But for now, no speeding, I mean it.'

'What do you mean? It was OK on the way here but not on the way back?'

'No arguments, Gallo. Just do as I say. Actually, give Catarella a buzz and tell him to tell everyone that I went to see Fazio and that he's doing well. That way, when we get back, nobody will come and bother me for information.'

*

'OK, Chief, here's the situation,' said Galluzzo, sitting down and pulling a sheet of paper out of his pocket. 'Vigàta has two chiropodists and one corn-and-callus specialist, and—'

'Aren't they the same thing?'

'No, sir, they're not. The Foot Boutique, which is one of the chiropody salons, has one sixty-year-old client, whose name I wrote down right here, with the address.

The other shop, called One Foot in Paradise, doesn't have any male customers.'

'And what about the corn-and-callus specialist?'

'He's got four clients around sixty, whose names and addresses I also took down.'

'Have you been to Montelusa yet?'

'Yesterday I wasted a good bit of time waiting for another callus specialist who was out plying his trade. I'm going back now.'

'All right. Send me Inspector Augello, and leave that sheet of paper with me.'

Montalbano showed Mimì the sheet as soon as he came in. Augello took it but didn't look at it.

'Did you talk to Fazio?'

'Yes.'

'What did he say?'

'Hardly anything at all. He said that someone by the name of Manzella, a former dancer he's known since primary school, had contacted him.'

'What did he want?'

'He wasn't able to tell me. Too weak. They broke up our meeting. I'm going back this afternoon at four.'

Mimì decided to look at the sheet of paper.

'Take my advice, go to the Boutique. I've been there a few times myself,' he said.

'Mimì, I'm not asking you to recommend a chiropodist to me. See that name written next to the Foot Boutique, and the other four written beside the name of the callus specialist? I want you to look up those five clients and talk to them.'

Augello was confused. 'Why?'

'Because Pasquano said that the first body we found at the well had very well-manicured feet.'

'Maybe he did his own pedicures at home.'

'And maybe not. If all five of these men are still alive, so much the better for them, and so much the worse for me. But if one of them's been missing for the past week, then we need to start investigating who he was and what he did. Got that?'

'Got it.'

'Best of luck.'

*

Now came the hardest part. He reviewed in his mind what he intended to say. He even recited one sentence – the most important – aloud, to hear how it sounded. When he felt properly ready, he reached out, picked up the receiver, and dialled Mr C'mishner's number.

NINE

He spoke in a faint, quavering voice, which to him was supposed to sound like that of a man at death's door.

'Montalbano here.'

'Yes, what is it?'

He audibly took a deep breath, then coughed softly twice.

'What is it, Montalbano?'

'I feel really, really baa . . .' Another little cough. 'I'm sorry, I'm having these regurgitations.'

'Montalbano, for heaven's sake!'

'You'll have to excuse me, but Dr Gruntz performed a super Scrockson on me. I couldn't wiggle out of it. I begged him to postpone it, but he wouldn't hear of it . . . So instead of a double, I got a super! Do you know what that means? He said I urgently needed one.'

'And what does it mean?'

'It means the effect of the super lasts double the double, so, until tonight, in other words.'

'I haven't understood a thing.'

'I'm unable to move.'

'Are you telling me you can't come this afternoon?'

'I'm terribly sorry, but . . .'

'Listen, Montalbano, either you will get here by your own means, or I'll send an ambulance to fetch you!'

'Mr Commissioner, sir, it's not a question of an ambulance, but of personal control . . . Do you understand?'

'No.'

'I don't dare get very far from a . . . er . . . place of relief –' how was it that when telling a lie, he often came up with fancy phrasings like that? – 'for more than five minutes. The super Scrockson is just ghastly, I can't think of any other word for it. Just imagine, I gave up a button I'd swallowed in 2001! And not just the button, but also—'

'Fine, I'll expect you at nine o'clock sharp, tomorrow morning,' said the commissioner, who was clearly about to vomit.

But how on earth could the commissioner swallow a tuppenny hoax like that? Perhaps because he considered the inspector a serious man, something of a pain in the arse, perhaps, but certainly not capable of such a thing. Montalbano didn't know whether to gloat or feel insulted. He left the question hanging and went to eat.

*

As he entered the trattoria, he felt reasonably hungry, owing in part to the fact that he'd liberated himself, however temporarily, from his visit to the commissioner.

'Listen, I just got a call on behalf of the commissioner,' Enzo said in a conspiratorial tone.

'Was he looking for me?' Montalbano asked, flabbergasted and angry.

So the commissioner hadn't believed him that he was laid up at home, suffering from the effects of the super Scrockson! Luckily Enzo answered in the negative.

'No, sir. He's going to be coming here to eat. He's got some friends with him who want to eat fresh fish. Reserved a table for six people.'

'When's he coming?'

'In about half an hour.'

Montalbano cursed the saints and shot to his feet as if he'd just sat on a viper. What if the commissioner caught him stuffing his guts with mullet and bream? Not only would he open an investigation, he would have him thrown off the police force! Then he really might have some sort of super Scrockson performed on him!

He made an immediate, and unavoidable, decision.

'I have to go.'

'And where are you going to eat?'

'Look, Enzo, I'd rather fast than see the commissioner.'

'Inspector, I can put you in the little room and not let anyone in!'

'But how am I going to leave after I've finished?'

'Don't you worry about that, I'll take care of everything. There's the back door.'

He'd just finished the spaghetti alle vongole when the door to the little room opened and Enzo poked his head in.

'They're here.'

Then he disappeared, only to return a few minutes later with the mullet. The inspector ate them with greater gusto than usual, precisely because he was enjoying them just a few yards away from the commissioner, who imagined he was at home shitting his soul out.

At two thirty sharp he left for Fiacca with Gallo. But in his own car, since that morning they'd all received a second reminder from the commissioner to economize on petrol.

*

Less than two miles out of town they ran into a roadblock of the carabinieri. There was a queue about ten cars long, stopped at the side of the road, the sort of thing that could waste half the day. Gallo pulled up at the end.

'Should we make ourselves known?' he asked.

'No,' said Montalbano.

Given the condition his car was in, if the carabinieri found out they were with the police, they would throw the book at him. He would have to pay a fine that even two months' pay wouldn't cover. A little while later, a corporal came up smiling, having seen who was at the wheel.

'Hello, Gallo.'

'Hello, Tumminello.'

Montalbano felt reassured. If those two were friends, they wouldn't lose any time answering their esteemed colleagues' questions.

'What's the roadblock for?' asked Gallo.

'We were ordered to look for and arrest a short, fat man with a scar on his left cheek, coming from the direction of Fiacca.'

The inspector felt like laughing. And he started talking to the corporal, lips smiling in a way that might be construed as mocking.

'Excuse me,' he said, 'but if you're supposed to stop someone coming from Fiacca, why stop us? We're going towards Fiacca! Perhaps you should all do an about-turn and start checking cars coming from the other direction. Otherwise this is like . . .'

He stopped himself in time. What the hell had made him open his big mouth? Meanwhile he noticed that Tumminello's expression had suddenly changed.

'And who are you?' the carabiniere asked.

'Ragionier Muscetta, a pleasure.'

'He's a dear friend of mine who asked me to do him a favour and . . .' Gallo tried to explain.

But the corporal wasn't listening and continued:

'Is this your car, Ragioniere?'

'Yes.'

'Please finish your sentence, Ragioniere.'

He was fixated on the ragioniere!

'What sentence? I didn't say anything that—'

'No, you said, "Otherwise this is like . . ." Now please finish.'

'Well, I just meant that otherwise, it's like . . . I dunno, it's like we're in a topsy-turvy world.'

'No, you were going to say, "Otherwise, this is like one of those carabinieri jokes." Isn't that right?'

'Come now, I would never dare to—'

'No, you wouldn't dare? Not even you, Inspector Montalbano, sir?'

Montalbano turned to ice.

'You can go,' said the corporal.

So he had recognized him at once and was only pulling his leg by calling him ragioniere! Meanwhile he had signalled to his colleagues to let the car through.

After they had been driving some ten minutes in silence, Montalbano said:

'I was of course about to say exactly what the corporal thought. Bright kid, that Tumminello.'

'He'll go far. He's doing a law degree.'

They passed another roadblock where, unlike the first one, it was cars coming from Fiacca that were being stopped.

'You see, I was right!' Montalbano said to Gallo. 'The first checkpoint was totally useless.'

'Chief, don't you know the story of Michele Misuraca, from about six months ago?'

'No.'

'Misuraca caught his married daughter with her lover. Since the husband was off in Germany, it was up to him to do something, and so he shot and killed the girl as her lover ran away. Misuraca got in his car and managed to get out of Fiacca just before the carabinieri put up the roadblocks. But then Misuraca returned and wasn't stopped by the carabinieri because they were only checking the cars coming out of Fiacca. So Misuraca went back into town without any trouble, tracked down the lover, killed him, then gave himself up.'

Montalbano made no comment.

Gallo made up for the time lost at the roadblock, and by a few minutes to four, the inspector found himself in the hospital's entrance lobby.

He took two steps and then stopped, seized by doubt. Was the lift to the left or the right?

'Inspector!'

He turned around. It was Angela, the nurse. The sight of her gladdened his heart.

'How very kind of you,' he said. 'I really wasn't expecting . . .'

'Expecting me to come? You're right, I wasn't going to, but then I changed my mind.'

'Why?'

'With all the confusion there's been here, I realized that without me, you'd never find your friend again.'

'Why, what confusion?'

'Around one thirty, after all the visitors left, a man, a stranger, was noticed on the fourth floor, poking around suspiciously, opening and closing doors as though looking for someone.'

'Sort of like me.'

'Yes, but when a nurse asks you a question, you don't run away with a gun in your hand.'

'Did he shoot?'

'No.'

'Was he caught?'

'They gave chase and saw him go out of the hospital, run across the car park, and disappear into the country-side.'

'Was he sort of short and fat?'

'Yes. How did you know that?'

'The carabinieri told me, at a roadblock. And what happened next?'

'The police had all the fourth-floor patients moved up to the sixth floor, which hadn't been opened yet and is a lot easier to keep under surveillance.'

Was it possible the man had come to kill Fazio? Possible, yes. After all, how many Mafiosi had been liquidated in their hospital beds? But Montalbano wanted to be sure.

'Were there any important patients on that ward?'

'The Honourable Frincanato and Judge Filippone, who

are from the Anti-mafia Commission. One with a broken leg, the other with a fractured pelvis. The car they were in crashed into an HGV. And they've received death threats.'

It was well known that there were plenty of doubts circulating about the supposed death threats received by Frincanato, whose statements held as much water as a bucket riddled with buckshot. Wicked rumours even had it that he wrote the anonymous letters himself to seem important. Judge Filippone, for his part, was someone who said yes when the majority said yes, and no when the majority said no. A puppet on strings. Imagine the Mafia risking one of their men to get one of those nobodies! Montalbano became worried, convinced that the gunman had come looking for Fazio.

When the lift opened on the sixth floor, the inspector found himself looking at two policemen armed with sub-machine guns. He immediately took out his badge, and they let him through. Outside rooms eight and ten were two more policemen with sub-machine guns.

Angela accompanied him as far as room fourteen.

'I wanted to let you know that I enquired and found out that Signor Fazio will be released in three days at the most. Tomorrow he'll be allowed to get up on his feet for a few hours.'

'That means you'll have to be my guide six more times.'

'You plan to come twice a day?'

'That's right.'

'The day after tomorrow it'll be hard for me to come to meet you.'

'Why?'

'Because I'll be on a shift in surgery. So you'll have to fend for yourself.'

'I'll manage,' said Montalbano. Then, out of the blue: 'May I invite you to dinner?'

Angela seemed neither surprised nor amazed. Beautiful as she was, she must have been used to being invited out all the time by men.

'Why?'

'To return the favour.'

Angela started laughing. Then she said: 'I'd be delighted to accept, but I already have an engagement . . . Nothing important, though. Could I give you a definite answer in a little bit? I'll make a phone call and try to free myself. If you don't see me here outside the door when you come out at four thirty, call me at this number.'

She wrote the number down on a piece of paper, which Montalbano put in his pocket. Angela chuckled again, then turned her back and started walking away. The inspector stood there for a moment, watching her from behind. It was a beautiful sight. Then he knocked on the door.

'Come in,' said a woman's voice.

*

The first thing he saw upon entering was the dwarf nurse, the Sing-Sing prison guard. Then he noticed that Fazio was not lying down, but sitting up, with pillows behind his shoulders and head. Mrs Fazio wasn't there.

'Seven minutes,' the bulldog nurse said right off the bat.

'You can't start counting until you've left the room,' Montalbano retorted. Then to Fazio, who was smiling and happy to see him, he said: 'Where's your wife?'

'I sent her home to rest,' the bulldog cut in, just as she was opening the door to go out. 'Our patient is now on the road to recovery.'

But before closing the door behind her, she repeated: 'Seven minutes!'

'Oh, fuck off,' Fazio said in a low voice.

'Speaking of which, I have some good news for you,' said Montalbano. 'Telling someone to fuck off is no longer a crime. As established by the Supreme Court of Appeals. Listen, do you know anything about what happened here at the hospital?'

'They told me there was someone trying to get into the rooms of two Anti-mafia officials.'

'Did they tell you who they were? Frincanato and Filippone.'

'But they're a couple of nobodies!' said Fazio, surprised.

'Exactly. So I'm not convinced.'

'Me neither.'

'Did he come to your room?'

'No.'

'Do you know anything about a short, fat guy with a scar on his left cheek?'

'Fuck!' Fazio shouted.

He turned pale as a corpse.

'Do you know him?'

'He was one of the men who wanted to kill me.'

'Just as I thought,' the inspector commented. And as Fazio was gesturing for him to hand him the glass of water on his bedside table, Montalbano continued:

'So the man came armed to the hospital just for you, to finish what he'd started.'

'Get me out of here!' Fazio exclaimed, handing him the empty glass.

'It's unlikely he will be back. Calm down.'

'Could I at least have a gun?'

'Are you crazy? That Sing-Sing nurse'll have you put in solitary!'

Fazio looked totally confused. 'Who are you talking about?'

'Never mind. Let's talk about what happened to you. It must have been a pretty big deal.'

'Chief, in all good conscience, I don't know whether it's a big or a small deal. When those two—'

'Wait. Let's start at the beginning. We'll break up the story in episodes, like they do on TV. Otherwise, at seven minutes a go, I'll never find out anything. Tell me about Manzella.'

Fazio thought about it for a moment, then began.

'Filippo Manzella and I went to primary school together here in Vigàta. Then we lost track of each other, his father worked with the railways and got transferred. But we met up again in the military. He was attending a dance school in Palermo, wanted to do classical ballet. And in fact he landed a job with the Teatro Massimo's ballet company. Every so often, when . . . I had to go to Palermo . . . we . . . we'd meet.' Fazio was already tired.

'Just rest now,' said the inspector.

Fazio closed his eyes and said nothing for about half a minute. He was about to resume talking, but couldn't manage.

'Then—' He broke off, breathing heavily.

'Just wait a little longer,' said Montalbano.

'No, I can't, the seven minutes'll be up. Then we lost track of each other again. One day I ran into him in Montelusa. He'd changed.'

'How?'

'He was fatter. And he wouldn't look me in the eye, not like he used to. He said he wasn't dancing any more, had got married, and that his wife was expecting. He said he didn't work any more and was living off an inheritance.'

He paused again. But by now his speech was laboured, with gaps between each word.

'About two weeks ago I ran into him again in Montelusa. He was in a hurry. All he did was ask for my mobile number. So I gave it to him, and then two days later, he called me.'

'What did he want?'

'He said he wanted me to look into something for him, said he thought it involved smuggling.'

'That's all he told you?'

'That's all.'

'Why didn't you say anything to me about it?'

'Chief, the whole thing seemed to me like some fantasy of his. Filippo used to like to make things up sometimes.'

'Go on.'

'So he kept calling me, saying he was being watched, that maybe they'd worked out that he was on to them . . . But whenever I asked if we could meet so he could tell me the whole story, he'd become evasive and start stammering . . .'

'Did you ever call him back after he'd called looking for you?'

'Yes. I had his mobile number.'

'Did you ever call him on a land line?'

'Yeah, but it was a bar. He likes to be mysterious . . .'

'Did he name any names?'

'Not one, he was always vague . . . And I got more and more convinced he was just talking rubbish.'

'All right, we haven't got much time left. Now just tell me why you went to the port.'

'After not phoning me for a few days, he rang. He said if I went there immediately I could catch them all red-handed. So I told my wife you'd called, and then I went out.'

'He never explained what kind of smuggling it was?'

'No. He only said he'd be waiting for me at the port, over by the warehouses, at three in the morning.'

'So why did you go out shortly after eight o'clock?'

'So the whole thing would seem more plausible to my wife.'

'Did you take your gun?'

'No.'

'Why the hell not?! You're going to meet a bunch of clearly dangerous smugglers and—'

'But I didn't want to meet them! I only wanted to see them without being seen. Then, before making any moves, I would've called for reinforcements. And you know what? I still didn't think any of it was real.'

'Time's up!' shouted the dwarf, coming in.

'One last question. The evening that Manzella called to tell you to come to the port, are you sure it was him on the phone?'

'It certainly sounded like him, though it's true the voice sounded far away and sort of garbled. He always called on the mobile. He said the reception wasn't very good.'

'All right, goodbye. See you tomorrow morning.'

TEN

Montalbano went out, but one second later he was back, reopened the door, and poked his head inside.

'I just remembered that I have to go and see the commissioner tomorrow morning. I'll see you in the afternoon.'

There was no sign of Angela in the corridor. It was exactly ten past four. He waited a few minutes, then went over to the policemen standing guard and held his badge up for them to see.

'I'm Inspector Montalbano.'

'Yes, sir,' they said in unison.

'One of your colleagues from the Vigàta police is in room fourteen. He suffered a wound to the head during a shoot-out. Could you keep a close watch over his door as well? It's not certain that the armed man who slipped into the hospital had come for the Anti-mafia officials. Have I made myself clear?'

'Absolutely, sir,' said one.

'Don't worry, we'll keep an eye on him,' said the other.

At the end of the corridor, he didn't know whether to turn right or left. Then he spotted, at the back of the hallway on the right, the two policemen with sub-machine guns standing guard in front of the lift. When he reached the ground floor, he took out the piece of paper Angela had given him. It was an internal number. He went up to the desk and asked one of the two women there to dial it for him. A moment later he was talking to Angela.

'I'm sorry, but I wasn't able to get free. Could we postpone everything till tomorrow?'

'That's perfectly fine with me.'

'All right, then, we can decide tomorrow morning on the time and place.'

'No, Angela, I can't come tomorrow morning.'

'Really?'

'Really. I have an engagement.'

'What about the afternoon?'

'I'll definitely be here at four in the afternoon.'

'OK, see you then. That way we can decide. My shift ends at six thirty.'

'Do you know a good place to eat here in Fiacca?'

'There are so many. But . . .'

'But?'

'I don't really want to be seen going out with . . . I mean, if somebody sees me with a stranger, there could be problems. Do you understand what I'm saying?'

'Perfectly.'

'It's not a problem for you?'

'Not at the moment, no. Want to come to Vigàta?'

'Sure, why not?'

She'd answered immediately. Clearly she had been expecting him to ask.

'Have you got a car?'

'Yes, but if you wait for about fifteen minutes after I get off, I can change here at the hospital, and we can go directly in yours.'

What on earth was going through the girl's head?

He simply wanted to invite her out to a dinner without consequences. But he was sure that whatever consequences there might be, he could dodge them without losing face.

The visitors' car park was behind the hospital complex, a good ten-minute walk away. The inspector found Gallo asleep, head thrown back and mouth open.

'Good morning!'

Gallo gave a start and opened his eyes. He looked a little disoriented.

'Sorry, Chief, I'm so behind on sleep, it's eatin' me alive.'

'You didn't sleep last night?'

'No, and I didn't the night before that, either. Soon as I lie down, I get this terrible stomach ache. And now I can't keep my eyes open.'

'Go and get yourself a coffee at the hospital bar.'

'I don't feel like it.'

'Listen, let's get something straight. I'm not going to

get in the car with someone who might suddenly fall asleep on a road full of traffic. I'll drive. You get in the back and get some sleep.'

Since he really did need to sleep, Gallo didn't protest. By the time the inspector had manoeuvred out of the car park, Gallo was already in a deep sleep.

As might be expected, the roadblock was still up outside Fiacca, and Montalbano's car was stopped. Seeing a man lying on the back seat with his arm over his face, the carabiniere grew suspicious. He'd started bending down to say something through the window, but then suddenly stood back, as though changing his mind. As he was calling a couple of his colleagues over for a look, the inspector decided to play a little trick on Gallo. The three carabinieri approached cautiously, hands on the hilts of their revolvers. Montalbano leaned back and enjoyed the scene, sitting motionless with his hands clearly visible above the steering wheel.

'What's he doing, sleeping?' the first carabiniere asked the inspector.

'Yeah. Deeply.'

'Wake him up.'

'Wake him up yourself. But I should warn you: he gets upset whenever somebody startles him awake. His reactions are unpredictable. So now I've told you, I don't want the responsibility.'

'So how should I wake him up?'

'I don't know. Try saying something sweet to him, stroke his cheek...'

'Come on, are you joking?'

'Do I seem like someone who likes a joke?' Montalbano replied, looking offended.

The carabiniere went to discuss matters with the other two officers, then said to the inspector: 'Please get slowly out of the car.'

'With my hands in the air?'

'There's no need.'

Montalbano got out without making the slightest noise.

The carabiniere then jerked open the back door, jumped aside, and yelled:

'You! Get out with your hands up!'

Gallo woke up with a start to find three guns pointed at him and started shouting.

'I'm a police officer! Don't shoot!'

'Let's see your papers.'

Gallo took them out, and the first carabiniere tore into Montalbano.

'Why didn't you tell us he was a policeman?'

'You didn't ask.'

The carabiniere called to the marshal. His superior wanted to see Montalbano's papers.

'Why didn't you identify yourself?' he asked.

'Nobody asked me to. This carabiniere simply asked

me if my officer was asleep. And I said yes. Is this going to take much longer?'

'No, Inspector. Just long enough to give you a fine. Is this your car?'

'Yes. Why?'

'You're driving with your lights off and a broken rear light.'

Just deserts for messing with the carabinieri and not letting Gallo drive.

*

When he got to his office, he found Mimì sitting there, waiting for him.

'What can you tell me?'

'Found them all.'

'What's that supposed to mean?' asked Montalbano, who at that moment was thinking about Angela.

'It means all five gentlemen around sixty who like to have their feet pedicured answered the call. I also checked the Montelusa phone book, which Galluzzo gave me. All alive and kicking. Therefore the victim did not go to any of the chiropodists in Vigàta or Montelusa. Nor did he have anything to do with the callus specialist. Fazio tell you anything?'

'Yes.'

The inspector told him about Manzella.

'And why did they shoot at him at the port?'

'I'll find that out in the next instalment.'

'I believe I heard you say Manzella told Fazio he was married and his wife was pregnant,' said Mimì.

'You heard right. And it's the only thing we've got to go on at the moment.'

Without saying a word, Augello got up, went out, and returned with the telephone book, which he started thumbing through.

'There are two Filippo Manzellas in Vigàta. And another in Montelusa,' he concluded from his search.

'Turn on the speakerphone and start with Vigàta.'

The first Filippo Manzella was a surly old man who started abusing Mimì. The second wasn't at home, a woman calling herself his wife assured him; he'd left about an hour earlier on a trawler.

'So we have to rule this one out, too, since at least until an hour ago, he was still alive,' Augello concluded.

Montalbano looked at him with an expression somewhere between admiration and astonishment.

'Mimì, you sometimes arrive at staggering conclusions that would put even Monsieur Lapalisse to shame.'

'I've learned from you,' Augello retorted, dialling the Montelusa number.

'Hello, who's there?' asked a female voice.

'Police,' said Mimì.

The woman got scared. 'Oh my God, what's happened?'

'Please don't be alarmed, signora. I'm just calling about a fine. Does Mr Filippo Manzella live there?'

'Not any more.'

'What do you mean?'

'I mean that my husband and I no longer live together. We separated five years ago.'

'I see. Do you know where he lives now?'

'Well, until about two weeks ago I knew he was living in Vigàta at Via della Forcella 13, but the last time he phoned me, he said he'd moved.'

'When was that?'

'As I said, about two weeks ago.'

'And he hasn't called since then?'

'No.'

'Aren't you worried that he hasn't contacted you?'

'No, I'm used to these silences. He only calls me for news of his son. But sometimes he'll go a whole month without calling.'

'Did he give you his new address?'

'No.'

At this point Montalbano took the phone away from him.

'Hello, signora, this is Chief Inspector Montalbano. Would you mind if I came to Montelusa to talk to you?'

'Right now?'

'Yes. Let's say in about half an hour.'

'No, I was just about to go out. If you want, you can come tomorrow morning any time after eleven.'

Montalbano thanked her, hung up, and rose.

'You coming with me?' he asked Augello.

'Where?'

'Wake up, Mimì! To Via della Forcella 13!'

*

Via della Forcella was in one of those recently built-up areas along the road to Montereale. Number 13 was a six-storey building, and beside the main entrance was a sign that said: APARTMENTS FOR RENT. SEE PORTER.

Montalbano parked, got out, and went in. Mimì had decided it was best for him to go in alone, after phoning Beba and learning that little Salvuzzo had taken a tumble and hurt his forehead.

Inside the porter's lodge, which was actually a studio flat, he looked through an open door and saw a woman busying herself with a broom.

'Is the porter here?'

'No.'

'Could you tell me who I should talk to for information on the available apartments?'

'Me.'

'And who are you, may I ask?'

'The concierge. Is that good enough?'

'It's good enough for me.'

But he really didn't feel like talking about Manzella with a woman who seemed like a busybody.

'Listen, do you know when your husband will be back?'

'If he can still find the way home, he should be back around eleven.'

'Does he have a job?'

'Yes.'

'Where?'

'At Gnazio Cutaja's shop. His job is to empty glass after glass of wine. Know what I mean?'

Witty, the concierge.

'I do.'

An alcoholic. It was hopeless; he had no choice but to talk to her. Meanwhile the woman had stopped and, leaning on the broomstick, was eyeing him with a hint of malevolence.

'Mind if I say something?' she asked.

'Go ahead.'

'You smell like a cop. No offence.'

It was best to lay his cards on the table.

'You're right. I'm an inspector.'

'Please come in and sit down.'

Montalbano sat down on one of the chairs around a small table. From a tiny little kitchen came a wonderful smell of fish soup.

'Would you like a little wine?'

'Please don't bother, thanks. My compliments on the fish broth, though. It must be delicious, to judge from the smell.'

The woman's attitude changed. She propped the broom up in a corner, smoothed out her apron, and sat down on one of the other chairs.

'Ask me anything. I can tell you whatever you want to know.'

'Signora, we've learned that a man named Filippo Manzella is supposed to have lived in one of the studio flats in this building until about twenty days ago. Is that correct?'

'Yes, sir. He's a good man.'

'How long did he live here?'

''Bout three years.'

'Why did he leave?'

'He said he found something better.'

'Did he leave a forwarding address?'

'No.'

'So what was he going to do about the post and bills?'

'He said he'd come by once a week.'

'When did he last come?'

'He never came. I put aside three letters for him and an electricity bill.'

'Did he ever receive visitors?'

'Not during the day.'

'How about at night?'

'Mr Inspector, how should I know? I lock up the lodge at seven thirty every night, have dinner, watch TV, and go to bed. Whoever wants to come in uses the intercom outside.'

'Could I have a look at the flat where he used to live?'

'What do you think you're going to find there? When

I cleaned it up, all's I found was a telescope he tol' me he'd come and pick up.'

'And where's this telescope?'

'It's still in the flat. Just the way he left it, 'cause it's not been rented yet.'

'Could I see it?'

The woman sighed, got up, went into the other room, returned with a set of keys, and handed them to the inspector.

'You can go by yourself. Sixth floor, number eighteen. Sorry, but I gotta look after my soup. There's a lift.'

*

The door opened directly onto a small sitting room endowed with a television niche and an alcove kitchen. The sitting room led into the bedroom, where there was barely enough room for a double bed, a tiny cupboard, two bedside tables, and a window. A narrow door led into a microscopic bathroom with a shower. There were two telephone jacks, one in the living room, one in the bedroom, but there was no sign anywhere of a functioning phone. The telescope was enormous: resting on a tripod, it took up half the sitting room. It was pointed towards the port of Vigàta. The moment the inspector brought his eye to the eyepiece, he felt as if he could touch the outer wall of one of the refrigerated warehouses on the side facing the sea, where the trawlers tied up to unload. The wide main door was open, and inside he could clearly see two men busy working. As he was leaving the studio flat, it suddenly occurred to him to look inside the cupboard. In addition to some blankets and a change of sheets, he found a pair of binoculars in their case. He took them out. They were powerful military binoculars with infrared lenses.

Manzella must have bought them on the black market for a hefty sum.

He put them back, closed up, went downstairs, and gave the keys back to the concierge.

'A few more questions and then I'll leave you in peace.'

'Go ahead.'

'Why didn't I see any telephones?'

'Mr Manzella used only a mobile phone.'

'Do you know where he worked?'

'He didn't.'

'So how did he get by?'

'I don't know. But he was never wantin' for money.'

'Did he ever go out?'

'Of course! Mornings, when he was here, he would go out grocery shopping 'cause he liked to cook while listening to music, he even had a big stereo, an' in the afternoons he'd sleep till five an' then—'

'Wait a moment. You said "when he was here". You mean he wasn't always here?'

'No, sir, he wasn't. Sometimes he'd disappear for weeks at a time.'

'Where'd he go?'

'How should I know?'

'Who normally cleans the apartments?'

'Me, my sister, an' my sister-in-law.'

'Who cleaned Manzella's place?'

'I did.'

'Here's a rather delicate question, signora. When you made his bed in the morning, did you ever get the impression that Manzella had slept with a woman?'

The concierge started laughing.

'The impression? Mr Inspector, sometimes it was like an earthquake had hit! Pillows on the floor, sheets all tangled, an' one time even half the mattress was on the floor.'

'Did that sort of thing happen often?'

'Lately, yes.'

'Was he a ladies' man?'

'What do you think, when you see a bed in that condition a good three nights a week?'

'Three nights a week? But isn't he getting on in years?'

'Yeah, but I guess it's still workin' pretty good. Or maybe he takes pills.'

'Was it always the same woman, or did he see a lot of different ones?'

'How am I supposed to know?'

'I don't know, by the colour of the hair on the pillow or in the shower...'

'Wouldja believe it? I never found a single hair!'

'How about a hairpin or some lipstick?'

'Nothin'.'

'How can that be?'

'Maybe they was careful.'

'Does Manzella have a car?'

'Used to.'

'What do you mean?'

'There's a Mr Falzone lives in the building who sells used cars. Manzella sold him his for pennies. A Fiat Panda in really good condition.'

'When did he do that?'

'A couple of days before leaving. He said he wanted to buy a new one.'

'How'd Falzone pay him?'

'Manzella wanted cash. I was there.'

'Where'd he put his belongings?'

'One suitcase was enough. He didn't own much. If you ask me . . .'

'Go on.'

'If you ask me, Manzella had another house.'

'One last thing. Could you give me the three letters?'

The concierge seemed undecided.

'An' what'll I tell Manzella if he comes by?'

'Tell you what. I'll leave you a receipt. That way, Mr Manzella can come and pick them up at the station.'

ELEVEN

While leaving the building, he was thinking that Manzella's departure was not a simple change of residence, but
looked a lot like the sudden flight of someone who wanted
to vanish without a trace.

He moved the car just enough to avoid arousing the
curiosity of the people in the building, then pulled over
and took the letters out of his pocket.

The first one had been sent from Palermo and was
signed, 'Your loving sister, Luciana.' It was one long
complaint: the ninety-year-old mother needed assistance;
Luciana's husband was a dissolute pervert; the son had
lost his head chasing after a girl who seemed like a saint
but in fact was a real slut, to the point that she made him
buy the panties she wore . . . In short, the sister was asking
for money.

The second letter was from a certain Sebastiano and
sent from Messina. He said things were going well, he'd
got his head straightened out and had finally found the

love of his life. Of whom he'd attached a photograph. It showed a young man in a naval uniform, about twenty-five years old, with a low brow, ears that stuck out, and a horsey face.

He must have been about six foot three and was so well built that he looked like an athlete, though his legs were so bowed they practically formed a circle.

Montalbano thought that love, as we know, is blind.

The third and last letter, posted in Vigàta, he read twice.

Then he drove off, dropped in at the station, and put the first two letters in a drawer of his desk and the third in his jacket pocket. Then he left and headed home to Marinella.

*

The night was soft and clear and windless. And the moon, instead of resting over the orchards, was floating on the sea. Autumn felt perhaps that its days were numbered and was surrendering to its end with a sort of melancholy and slightly distracted languor, letting itself be invaded, without resistance, by days and nights already springlike. Sitting out on the veranda, Montalbano had wolfed down a huge dish of *pasta 'ncasciata* that Adelina had left for him in the oven. Normally it was a lunch dish, but luckily his housekeeper had never made any distinction between things that were better for lunch and things that were better for dinner. And sometimes the inspector suffered the consequences. As would certainly be the case that night, since digesting *pasta 'ncasciata* sometimes led to nocturnal battles. Sighing, he stood up, went into the house, and sat down at the table, on which he'd left the letter addressed to Filippo Manzella, and read it for the third time.

> *Ippo,*
>
> *Would you please tell me why you suddenly don't want to see me any longer?*
>
> *I've tried to reach you dozens of times on your mobile, but you won't ever answer. Why? I think someone may have told you wicked things about me, totally invented lies, and you, silly man, believed them. The Fiacca story, if they told you about it, was nothing. Aside from the fact that I miss you, I think we absolutely need to meet and clear things up. There could be consequences. It's in your own interest. Get it?*
>
> *So give me a ring. G.*

The first problem presented by the letter, which was sent from Vigàta to another address in Vigàta and written in perfect Italian, was in the final lines, where there was a menacing shift in tone. If Manzella wanted to break things off with his girlfriend G, why did G write that there could be consequences? At any rate, it was clear that Manzella stood to lose everything from these 'consequences'. Was it to avoid such unpleasant consequences that Manzella had fled his flat without leaving a forwarding address? By the same token, he must have sold the car so that nobody could trace the licence plate back to the owner.

The second problem was that the letter didn't quite add up. The overall tone didn't make sense. Nothing indicated with any certainty that G was a woman, since the handwriting could have been either feminine or masculine. And a woman who'd just been abandoned by a man with whom she'd had a relationship would have used different, somewhat more passionate words. But if it was a man . . . Would a man have ever used expressions like 'wicked things'? Or 'silly man'?

What would he, Montalbano, have written? He thought of words like rubbish, crap, slander, gossip . . . No, 'wicked things' was not something a man would say. Nor was 'silly man' a manly expression. It was probably best to take the letter with him when he went to Montelusa Central. He could ask Gargiùlo in the Forensics department, who was a good handwriting analyst, for help.

The inspector went to bed after a long telephone conversation with Livia, which ended on a positive note. But he had an infernal night, all because of the *pasta 'ncasciata*.

*

'You look a little pale today. Everything all right in the bosom of the family?' asked that colossal pain in the arse

Dr Lattes, chief of the commissioner's cabinet, who never set foot outside his boss's waiting room and was always there, ready to torment every poor wretch who entered.

'Everyone's fine, with thanks to the Blessed Virgin.'

'His honour the commissioner is waiting for you.'

He'd been very punctual. Bonetti-Alderighi seemed solicitous, and even stood up.

'My dear Montalbano! Please sit down. How are you? All better now? You look a little pale.'

Of course he was pale! He hadn't slept a wink because of the pasta 'ncasciata!

'Well, the after-effects of the super Scrockson are devastating, since the tube is inserted into—'

'For heaven's sake, spare me the details. Anyway, I don't want to tire you out. Just tell me what happened.'

'Mr Commissioner, sir, I have very little to tell you, which is why I didn't file a report. In a few words, I received an anonymous tip concerning some suspected drug traffic passing through the port and sent Inspector Fazio to go and check it out. As far as we know, as soon as he got there, he was shot and wounded in the head, and then disappeared. Later we learned, from an anonymous phone call, that Fazio had been seen with two men in the area of the three wells. They intended to kill him. I called the fire department, and they pulled two corpses out of two different wells, but Fazio was still nowhere to be found.'

'Did you inform the prosecutor of these discoveries?' the commissioner interrupted.

'Of course. And Forensics and Dr Pasquano as well. All in order.'

'And then what?'

'Then Fazio was spotted on the road to Fiacca.'

'Who spotted him?'

'A . . . colleague from the police department there who knew him.'

'Go on.'

'Fazio was wandering about. I caught up with him, but he didn't recognize me, so I took him to the hospital in Fiacca, where he's still a patient. They had to operate.'

'Have you gone to see him? Has he told you anything?'

'I haven't gone there yet, because the doctors told me, over the phone, that he hasn't recovered his memory yet. He can't remember anything at all. It's going to take some time.'

'Are the doctors sure his memory will return to full function?'

'Absolutely.'

They talked for another ten minutes, then the commissioner said: 'Keep me informed.'

Which meant that the discussion was over. Montalbano had told him a blend of lies and truth but, more importantly, he had managed, with the story of Fazio's amnesia, to make sure that nobody would bother him at the hospital. All in all, however, the commissioner, perhaps worried he might aggravate the effects of the super Scrockson if he was mean to Montalbano, had been rather understanding.

The inspector went to the Forensics lab, hoping not to run into the chief, Vanni Arquà, whom he didn't like. He didn't see him anywhere, but neither did he see Gargiulo.

'Looking for someone, Inspector?' asked a youngster from the staff.

'Yes, Gargiulo.'

'He's not coming in today. Try again tomorrow.'

'Could you do me a favour?'

'Sure.'

Montalbano took G's letter to Manzella out of his pocket.

'Could you give him this for me and ask him to have a look at it? Tell him I'll give him a ring tomorrow.'

*

He went out of the building. There was a bar just around the corner. He ordered an espresso, and as they were making it, he checked the telephone book. Filippo Manzella lived at Via Croce 28. That is, on the opposite side of town. Going there by car was out of the question. Montelusa was a labyrinth of streets and alleys forever broken up by roadworks and the one-way system. He decided to go to Via Croce on foot, nice and slow, since

he had all the time in the world. The appointment with
Mrs Manzella wasn't till eleven.

*

The apartment was on the fifth floor of a tall eight-storey
building. It was small but sparklingly clean and in perfect
order.

Mrs Manzella sat him down in the living room and
asked if he'd like some coffee. Montalbano declined,
asking only for a glass of water. The walk there had been
long and all uphill.

The lady, who told him her name was Ernestina, was
nice-looking, about forty-five, primly dressed, and must
have been a pretty girl in her youth. And she seemed like
a thinking person. It was she who opened the discussion.

'Now tell me sincerely,' she said, 'this story of the fine,
you completely made that up, didn't you?'

Montalbano breathed a sigh of relief. It was better to
show his hand.

'Yes. How did you know?'

'A police inspector isn't going to bother to come all
the way to my apartment for a simple traffic ticket.'

Montalbano smiled and said nothing.

'What's happened to Filippo?' Mrs Ernestina asked.
But she didn't seem particularly worried.

'We don't know.'

'Then why are you interested in him?'

'Because he's disappeared.'

Ernestina smiled.

'But the man is always disappearing! It's an innate habit of his! A week, two weeks, a month! Even during our first year of marriage he would sometimes tell me he had to leave the next day without saying where, and he would vanish. And the whole time he was away, he never phoned me, not even once.'

'Did you ever ask him why he went away?'

'Of course! Hundreds of times! And without fail, he would say it was "for business".' But I never believed it. You want my advice? Stop looking for him. You'll see, sooner or later he'll turn up.'

'Signora, I think the problem is a lot more complex than that.'

'What do you mean?'

'I can't really tell you anything right now, but I came here because I need to ask you a few questions.'

'All right, go ahead.'

'When did the two of you get married?'

'Eighteen years ago.'

'Were you in love with each other?'

'It seemed like love at the time.'

'If I remember correctly, you said you have a son.'

'Yes, Michele. He's in his third year of high school.'

'As far as you know, have Michele and his father continued to see each other since the separation? What I mean is, to see each other of their own free will, beyond the prearranged meetings.'

'Up until his second year in high school, they saw each other often. Sometimes Filippo would pick him up after school. But then Michele didn't want to see him any more.'

'Why not?'

'He wouldn't tell me. He said they'd had a fight. But, at any rate, I was pleased.'

'Why?'

'I was always worried Filippo might have a bad influence on him.'

'In what sense?'

'When he was young, Filippo was a ballet dancer. Do you know what it means here when people say someone's a dancer?'

'Yes, it means he's fickle, whimsical, moody . . .'

'That's exactly right: fickle. Filippo was fickle in everything: friendship, affection . . . and even little things. His preferences would change overnight. He'd be crazy for ice cream, and then one day he'd stop eating it and claim he'd never liked it. It really wasn't easy living with him.'

'What did he do for a living when you got married?'

'He was a clerk at the Town Hall. He had a decent salary, enough to live on. Nothing lavish, mind you, but anyway . . . He worked there for five years. It was like he'd turned over a new leaf.'

'Then what happened?'

'Then his father's brother died, Uncle Carlo, and left him everything he had, which was rather a lot.'

'Why all to him?'

'Filippo never talked to me about Uncle Carlo, and I never met him. He didn't even come to our wedding.'

'How many brothers and sisters does your ex-husband have?'

'Two sisters. One of them, Luciana, has stayed in touch with him, always asking for money. The other one, Elvira, I don't know anything about.'

'What did this inheritance consist of?'

'Mostly houses, shops, warehouses, and a very well-functioning farm.'

'Excuse me, but isn't it possible your husband's constant trips had something to do with these business concerns?'

Ernestina smiled again.

'Are you kidding? Do you really think Filippo wanted those kinds of problems? He sold everything and put all the money in the bank.'

'Which bank?'

'More than one. At the one bank I knew about, the Banca Cooperativa, both our names were on the account. He would put in enough money for us to get by each year. I have no idea where he kept the rest of it.'

'What led to the breakup?'

'He started losing interest in me. Completely, if you know what I mean. I was nobody for him any more. Or, rather, I was the mother of his son, but as a woman, I was nothing. I wasn't there. I believe that was when he began to cheat on me and have a number of different lovers.'

'How did you find out?'

'I didn't. I said: "I believe". But he started doing the usual things that I'm sure you know all about.'

'I'm not married, signora.'

'Oh. Well, mysterious phone calls, vague appointments, contradictions, non-existent meetings. That sort of thing. In the end I got fed up and kicked him out. And there you have it.'

'In that Vigàta apartment you mentioned to us, we found an enormous telescope.'

Ernestina showed no surprise.

'It was one of his manias.'

'Did he look at the stars?'

Ernestina gave a long laugh. 'Would you come with me, please?'

She stood up, and the inspector followed her into the bedroom. The window looked out onto a courtyard with a great many balconies and windows large and small giving onto it.

'Have you ever seen that film where a man with a broken leg spends his days spying on other people through the window?'

'*Rear Window*, Hitchcock.'

'My husband used to do the same thing. I would watch television, and he would watch what others were doing in their homes.'

'And what did he tell you?'

'About what?'

'About what the others were doing in their homes.'

'Ah, well! That was all he ever wanted to talk about. The newlywed bride ushering her lover into the house was his favourite character. Another favourite was the old pensioner who would sneak into his granddaughter's room the moment his wife fell asleep. But I wouldn't give him the satisfaction – I really don't like that sort of thing.'

'I'm sorry, signora, but I have to ask you a difficult question. When he did these things, did he always remain only an observer?'

Ernestina must not have grasped the real meaning of the question.

'Why? What else could he do?'

'You know, sometimes in cases like this, the desire to intervene, to upset the normal course of other people's lives, becomes very strong. It's hard to resist the temptation.'

Ernestina finally got it. 'You mean blackmail?'

'Yes, but not only. You can also intervene just for fun.'

'How?'

'Let me give you an example. I see the young housewife letting her lover into the apartment, and so I write an anonymous letter to the husband and then sit back and enjoy what happens next.'

'You call that fun?'

'No, I don't, personally, but some people might.'

Ernestina paused to think about this for a few

moments, opened her mouth to speak, closed it again, then finally spoke.

'I really don't think Filippo would ever be capable of blackmailing someone. I suppose he might do something just for the wicked fun of it. But he wasn't a bad person inside, you shouldn't think that. You've never met him. He's . . .'

'Well, it's precisely because I've never met him that I'm asking you these questions. You were saying he's . . .'

'Unpredictable, that's it.'

They returned to the living room. But Montalbano didn't sit down again.

'Pardon me for asking, signora, but do you live on what your ex-husband gives you, or do you work?'

'Afternoons I work as a sales assistant in a clothes shop. And I have a gentleman friend. We're going to get married as soon as the divorce is settled.'

She said this without hesitation, and Montalbano appreciated her sincerity.

'Then I guess I have nothing more to ask you. I'll be on my way. But if by any chance your husband gets in touch with you, please call me at once at Vigàta police. You've been very kind.'

'I'll show you out.'

As Montalbano was descending the first stair and Ernestina was closing the door, he suddenly wanted to ask her another question, something that had been left hanging.

'I'm sorry, signora, but you said that the telescope was one of your husband's manias. What were the others?'

'He had one other: his feet. He was constantly fussing over them.'

A bolt of lightning paralysed the inspector. He stood there with his body half rotated, head turned all the way around, left foot raised above the second stair, right hand gripping the banister. He couldn't move. Signora Ernestina got worried.

'Inspector, do you feel all right?' she asked, coming out onto the landing.

'Wha . . . wha . . .' Montalbano stammered. Then he caught his breath and managed to speak.

'Why did your husband give up dancing?'

'He had an accident. He ruptured a ligament.'

Montalbano very nearly rolled down the stairs.

*

'And so, if Manzella had been in the well for five days, the phone call to Fazio was a trap.'

'Jesus, Mimì, you're getting so sharp you're becoming dangerous!'

'You told me Fazio didn't believe what Manzella was telling him. Whereas it was all true.'

'Another staggering conclusion, Mimì.'

'Salvo, you know what I say to you? I'm just going to stop talking. I'm sick of this bollocks.'

'Let me ask you a question. That way you'll be forced

to say something a little less idiotic. In your opinion, why did they shoot one of his feet?'

'One of whose feet?'

'Manzella's. Didn't I tell you? No? First they shot him in the foot, then they let him bleed for a few hours, and in the end they killed him. The question is: why?'

'To make him talk.'

'All right, Mimì, but that's not what I'm asking. Why in the foot? Normally to make somebody talk, you burn his hand with a cigarette or you shoot him in the knee or the arm...'

'Maybe the gun went off by accident.'

'You're cold, Mimì.'

'Maybe he had a thing about his feet, maybe he took good care of them...'

'You're getting warmer, Mimì.'

'Because he used to be a ballet dancer!'

'Bravo, Mimì! You see? When you put your mind to it, you can be intelligent! They shot him in the part of his body he cared most about. To humiliate him.'

TWELVE

Mimì was lost in thought.

'What is it?'

'I just remembered a movie I saw many years ago. A Western. Some bandits shoot someone in the foot to . . . No, Salvo, they didn't do it to humiliate him. They wanted to have fun with him. He raised the injured foot while the others shot around his good foot, telling him to dance. And he jumped around . . . turning round in circles . . . hopping and jumping . . .' He trailed off.

'Salvo, what's wrong?' he said.

Montalbano had turned very pale. The seagull's dance of death had suddenly come back to him.

'It's nothing . . . Just a little dizziness.'

'Do you ever have your blood pressure taken?'

'We were talking about something else entirely, Mimì. Please continue.'

'Well, apparently with their game they got him to talk, maybe by telling him they would spare his life. And so he told them he'd mentioned a couple of things to Fazio, and they killed him.'

'And then they tried to liquidate Fazio.'

'So what do we do now?' Augello asked.

'Two urgent things. First, we have to get Fazio to a safe place. Somewhere nobody knows about.'

'Got any ideas?'

'There's something I want you to do. Go to the commissioner, right now, and tell him the whole story of Manzella, and tell him also that they've already tried to get at Fazio in Fiacca Hospital.'

'Shall I ask him for round-the-clock surveillance?'

'No. I want Fazio brought to one of our own infirmaries.'

'All right, but in the meantime?'

'I'm going to see him again today, and I'll try to stay as long as possible. I've also talked to the two officers keeping guard just a few yards down from his room. I think we can rest easy tonight.'

'And what's the second thing?'

'Do you remember Rizzica, who came to tell us his suspicions about the crew of one of his trawlers?'

'Of course I remember him.'

'Have him come in tomorrow, around noon. We've been wasting time. We should've listened to him sooner. Oh, and one more thing. You should probably inform Signora Ernestina.'

'Who's she?'

'Manzella's ex-wife.'

'Oh, what a pain. She's going to start crying, tearing her hair out, and I can't stand—'

'Calm down, Mimì. They've already filed for divorce, and she's with a new man who wants to marry her. You couldn't possibly give her better news. Also, bring her in to identify him.'

'But he's totally unrecognizable!'

'Mimì, first of all, a woman who's been married to a man for eighteen years will be able to identify him. Second, it's rather in her interest to identify him, believe me.'

'All right, I'm off to the commissioner's.'

*

The inspector ate lightly at Enzo's. Skipping the pasta, he had only a few antipasti and three fried mullets. He got back to the office just after two o'clock.

'Listen, Cat, I'm going to Fiacca. I'm taking my mobile, since I won't be back this evening. You can give me a ring if you need me. Otherwise I'll see you tomorrow morning.'

As he was heading towards the car park, he ran into Gallo.

'I'm ready, Chief.'

'I'm going to Fiacca alone, thanks.'

'Why? Look, I'm not tired any more! I had a good sleep last night.'

'You can drive me there tomorrow morning, all right?'

＊

He wasted time parking the car the way he wanted in the hospital car park. He needed it to be almost hidden behind all the others, almost impossible to find. Taking his pistol out of the glove compartment, he put it in his pocket, then began the ten-minute walk to the main entrance. When he got there, it was twenty past four. Angela was nowhere to be seen, which meant that he would have to find Fazio's room on his own. This time, however, it was relatively easy, since the two police guards were still posted outside the sixth-floor lift. He showed them his badge. Two other policemen stood outside the doors of the two Anti-mafia officials, but they weren't the same as the previous day. He knocked lightly at the door of room fourteen, but nobody answered. He knocked again. Nothing. So he turned the handle and went in.

The room was empty, the bed remade. No trace of Fazio's things anywhere. He went back out, closed the door, and approached the two policemen, badge in hand.

'I'm Inspector Montalbano. Do you know whether they've moved the patient from room fourteen somewhere else?'

'Yes, they have. About an hour ago. He was on a stretcher with his face all bandaged. There was a woman next to him, holding his hand.'

Montalbano felt a twinge in his heart. Want to bet Fazio had some sort of complication?

'Where'd they take him?'

'They didn't tell us.'

All he could do was go and ask at the information desk. He took the lift down to the ground floor.

'Listen, there was a friend of mine on the sixth floor who—' he started to say to the woman who was a little older than him.

She cut him off.

'Are you Inspector Montalbano?'

'Yes.'

'Professor Bartolomeo is expecting you.'

'Is he serious?' Montalbano asked, starting to sweat.

'Who?'

'My friend.'

'I have no idea.'

'Do you know where they've taken him?'

'I repeat: I have no idea. Talk to the professor.'

'Where can I find him?'

'Wait just a minute.'

She picked up the phone, muttered a few words, then hung up.

'Fourth floor, room two.'

Naturally, he took the wrong lift, turned down the wrong corridor, went to the wrong room. Then, by some miracle, he knocked on the right door. Bartolomeo was about sixty, tall and elegant, with a cordial manner. Seeing the inspector come in, he stood up from behind his desk.

'How is Fazio?' Montalbano asked immediately.

'Quite well.'

'Then why . . . ?'

'Please sit down, Inspector. I'll explain everything. A little over an hour ago, I got a phone call from Commissioner Bonetti-Alderighi, who's a friend of mine. He told me the patient was in grave danger and asked me to put him in a safe place until he could be moved to a police infirmary. And to keep the transfer as secret as possible. So I went and moved him myself. I wrapped his face so that he couldn't be recognized, and then, with the help of his wife and the nurse watching over him—'

'The surly one?'

'Yes. They should all be like her! As I was saying, with the help of his wife and the nurse, I took him to one of the three rooms in the attic that'll serve as guest rooms when they're finished. The door to the attic is locked, and the nurse has the key. Can't get any safer than that! Naturally the commissioner told me to let you know as soon as you got here.'

'Thank you, Professor, you're very kind. If you would explain how to get to the attic . . .'

'I'll alert the nurse that you're on your way, so she can open the door when you ring. Now let me explain how you get there. It's very easy.'

He explained, and Montalbano didn't understand a damn thing. But he felt too embarrassed to ask for further explanations, so he just thanked the doctor, said goodbye, and left.

All right, let's think about this calmly and coolly, he said to himself. *Logically speaking, 'attic' means the area above the top floor. Therefore, to get to the attic, one must first reach the sixth floor in this case. That is, go where I was before.*

He got there without any problem. To the sixth floor, that is. The two policemen recognized him and let him pass. But then the trouble began. After spending about half an hour exploring every corridor and opening and closing every door on the sixth floor under the increasingly suspicious gaze of the two policemen, who must have been asking themselves if this inspector was really an inspector, he had to surrender to the bitter reality: there was no staircase or lift leading from there to the attic. He went back down to the ground floor and immediately saw Angela talking to a man. She spotted him, too, and gestured to him to wait. Then, taking leave of the man, she came towards the inspector, smiling.

'Same old story?'

'Yeah.'

'Can't find the sixth floor?'

'Well, the fact is that—'

He broke off. Apparently Angela didn't know that Fazio had been moved. And he couldn't tell her. The fewer people knew about it, the safer Fazio would be. So how was he going to wriggle out of this? Angela herself came to his aid.

'Wait, I think I heard that Professor Bartolomeo had him moved.'

'Oh, really?'

'Yes.'

'And do you know where they moved him to?'

'I can find out. Wait a moment.'

Angela went over to the information desk, spoke to the elderly woman, then came back towards him, still smiling.

'Follow me. So, how shall we arrange things for later?'

'You tell me.'

'I don't want to be seen leaving the hospital with you.'

'What time did you say you get off work?'

'At six thirty. I'll be ready by six forty-five at the latest.'

'Listen, I have an idea. I'll give you my car keys. The registration number is BC 342 ZX. You can leave the building on your own and get in my car. I'll join you a few minutes later. All right?'

'All right. Here we are,' she said, stopping in front of a lift at the end of an endless corridor. Over the door was a sign that said: OUT OF ORDER! DANGER!

'But it's broken!' said Montalbano.

'Don't worry, it's not.'

She pushed a button and the door opened.

'This,' said Angela, 'is the lift that goes directly to the

attic. There's only one door on the landing. Just ring the bell. See you later.'

*

He rang the bell and immediately heard the voice of the Alcatraz prison guard.

'Who is it?'

'Montalbano.'

The inspector could feel himself being watched through a spy-hole. The door then opened onto a corridor.

'First door on the right,' said the prison guard. 'Ten minutes.'

Fazio was no longer in bed. Dressed in some sort of pyjamas and slippers, he was on a balcony with a view of the sea. His bandages had been reduced by half.

'Where's your wife?' Montalbano asked.

'She left just a minute ago. Would you please tell me what's going on?'

'We had to put you in a safe place.'

'Why?'

'Did you know we found two bodies in the wells?'

'Two? The only one I knew about was the man I threw down there myself.'

'I thought it was you who did that.'

'Yeah. Two of them grabbed me to throw me in, but then the one with the gun put it down on the edge. I don't know how I did it, but all of a sudden I shoved him with all my might, and he was teetering with his body half in and half out, when he lost his balance and fell in. So I grabbed the gun. The other man, the one with the scar, started running away. I fired at him but missed. It was terrifying, I tell you. I couldn't remember who I was, what I was doing there...'

'We'll talk about all that another time. So, as I was saying, when we were looking for you, we found the first body. This morning I realized it was your friend Manzella. His body had been there for at least five days.'

Fazio turned pale.

'So you think they're going to keep trying to kill me too?'

'How can you have any doubt about it? Didn't the man with the scar come looking for you here at the hospital? Did you think he came just to find out how you were doing? Tomorrow or the day after, the commissioner's going to have you moved to one of our infirmaries. That way we can all relax a little. Meanwhile, here's this.'

He handed him a pistol. Fazio put it under the pillow.

'Careful not to let the nurse see it, or she'll take it away from you.'

'I'll hide it better later.'

'I have to ask you something important. So think it over before answering.'

'Go ahead.'

'Did Manzella by any chance tell you where he was living in Vigàta?'

175

'Yes. There was one time he wanted me to come to his place, and he gave me the address. Then he changed his mind. But at the moment I can't remember it.'

'Maybe Via della Forcella?'

Fazio didn't hesitate.

'No, Chief, that's not it. It's ... it's ...'

'Don't force yourself, it'll come back to you. Do you still remember my mobile-phone number?'

'Yes.'

'If it comes back to you, call me right away, no matter what time of day, even tonight. Now I want you to calmly tell me everything, from the moment they shot you to what happened later.'

Fazio told him.

Leaving his house well before the hour of his appointment with Manzella, and not yet having eaten when he'd received the phone call, he'd gone to a trattoria and taken his time. In fact he'd even indulged in a couple of games of *tressette* and *briscola* with some friends he'd run into at the restaurant. Then, after midnight, he went to the port and started walking back and forth along the central quay in the area of the refrigerated warehouses. It was the nightly period of great activity. The trawlers were putting in and unloading their catch, then leaving, as the fish-laden refrigerated trucks also left. He walked until his legs hurt, but there was no sign of Manzella. Around three thirty in the morning, when there was hardly anyone left, he decided to go home. As he was walking past the slipway, he heard a gunshot, and immediately the bullet whizzed past him a few inches away. He couldn't go any further, or he would have come even closer to the person who had fired at him. So he turned around and started running towards the warehouses, and he could hear the gunman chasing after him.

'Was there anyone around?'

'I think I saw a few people.'

'And nobody came to your aid?'

'Are you kidding?'

'Go on.'

His intention, Fazio resumed, was to get to the end of the quay and take cover inside the pilots' building. But he never made it there, because a second shot grazed him in the back of the neck, and he fell down, hitting his head against a rock. He woke up briefly inside one of the refrigerated warehouses, but the refrigeration wasn't functioning.

'Rizzica's warehouse.'

'I don't know him.'

'I do. Go on.'

Later, he'd woken up again, this time at the bottom of a boat, which was surely taking him from the central quay to the western one.

'I still don't understand why they put me in a boat.'

'I'll tell you why. Because it would have been too dangerous to put you in the boot of a car. Sometimes the Customs officer on duty makes them open it.'

Later he'd realized he was inside a car. At another point they punched him awake and made him start walking. There were two of them.

They came to a drinking trough, and one of the two started beating him, wanting to know what Manzella had told him. But Fazio couldn't even remember who this Manzella was. In fact, he didn't even know who he was himself.

In the end they brought him to a well with the intention of throwing him in. After the scuffle that left one man in the well and the other running away from Fazio's bullets, he'd heard the sound of a car starting up. And then he'd started walking, not knowing where to go, and ended up at a tunnel. He went inside, but soon afterwards he heard a car come in, which had to be the other guy following him. And he shot at it. Later he woke up in a hospital.

'Nobody followed you into the tunnel in a car.'

'I swear there was—'

'The car in the tunnel was one of our squad cars, with Gallo at the wheel and me beside him.'

'So I shot at you?'

'You certainly did. Luckily you weren't feeling too good and you missed.'

'*Matre santa!*' said Fazio. 'I could have killed you!'

The door opened. It was the guard.

'Time's up.'

'As soon as it comes back to you, call me with that address. Don't forget.'

*

In the lift, the inspector looked at his watch. What with one thing and another, it was almost six. There was a bar on the ground floor. He sat down at a table. Visiting hours now being over, there wasn't anyone around.

'Can I get you something?' asked the barman. 'We're closing in half an hour,' he added. Apparently the waiter had already left.

'Yes, a J&B, neat.' Montalbano went over to the bar to get it, then drank it in small sips, to make the time pass. At the third sip, he felt a wave of melancholy wash over him.

'*If you don't feel up to it, have someone ring Angela, invent some excuse, and go home,*' said Montalbano Two.

'*Angela's got nothing to do with it, nothing whatsoever,*' said Montalbano One.

'*Come on! Angela is the primary cause of this melancholy, and you know it!*' Montalbano Two retorted.

At six twenty-nine he paid and went outside. He started pacing back and forth, smoking three cigarettes in a row. Then he headed slowly for the car park, now half empty, to the point where his car, which he'd parked behind all the others, was now sitting all by itself. There didn't seem to be anyone inside, but when he got a little closer, he saw the gleam of Angela's blonde hair. She was in the passenger's seat, leaning all the way forward so that no one could see her face.

*

'You can drop the formal address with me.'

'Then you do the same with me.'

'I hope you don't mind, but it wouldn't feel right to me.'

'Why not?'

'There's too big a difference ...'

'In age?'

'No! Of course not! I was going to say there was too big a difference ... well, in status.'

'You mean social status?'

'Exactly.'

'Do you think that matters?'

'Of course it matters!'

'Listen, Angela. Imagine for a moment that I'm a patient in your care and very ill. Would you use the familiar or formal address with me?'

'Um ... I dunno, maybe the familiar.'

'You see? Now imagine I'm on death's doorstep.'

Angela laughed. 'All right, I give up. But don't think I'm going to want to play doctor with you.'

She said it half seriously, half in jest. And this time it was Montalbano who laughed.

THIRTEEN

'Do you have any problems about dinner?'
'What do you mean?'
'Can you eat everything, or are you on a diet?'
'I eat everything and always have a good appetite.'
'Do you like fish?'
'I love fish.'
'Do you mind if I smoke?'
'No. In fact, I'd like one myself.'

*

'What time are you going to work tomorrow?'
'Tomorrow I'm on the afternoon to evening shift.'
'So you can stay out late tonight.'
'Absolutely.'
She gave a hint of a smile.

*

'I seem to have the impression you don't have a boy-friend.'

'I did until a few days ago.'

She said it in a tone of voice that made Montalbano prick his ears up.

'Who broke it off?'

'He did.'

'How did he have the courage?'

'I don't understand.'

'It would take a lot of courage to leave a girl like you. Were you in love with him?'

'Yes.'

'But he wasn't in love with you.'

'But he was!'

'So why did you break up?'

She clearly wasn't too keen on discussing the subject. Montalbano realized he'd touched a sore spot.

'Things don't...' she began.

'Go on.'

'Things don't always depend on what we want.'

He had to press on.

'You mean he was forced somehow to leave you?'

'Yes.'

'Can't you do anything to change his mind?'

'He can't change his mind.'

'You must insist!'

'But you don't understand...'

She said it with a note of desperation in her voice.

He'd been right on target. But he tried to make it look like he'd missed the mark. 'Did he marry another girl?'

'I wish! Please, let's talk about something else.'

'You're crying! I'm so sorry, please forgive me. I had no idea...'

He was an utter swine. He'd forced her to tears and was now pretending not to have realized the sort of result his questions would have.

*

'Where are you taking me?'

'To a seaside restaurant where they give you so much fish for antipasti that I advise you to skip the first course.'

'Sounds fantastic! How far away is it?'

'Another half an hour and we'll be there.'

'Is it near your house?'

'Ten minutes.'

'Do you have a beautiful house?'

'It's the location that's beautiful. There's a veranda that leads on to the beach, and I like to spend hours on end just sitting there.'

'Will you take me to see it, afterwards?'

'If you like.'

'We can have a whisky on the veranda.'

*

'I'm sorry about your friend, but I'm glad it gave us the opportunity to meet each other. How's he doing?'

'He's getting better by the minute.'

Your move, Angela.

'They said he lost his memory. Is that true?'

Not bad for an opening gambit.

'Unfortunately, yes.'

Back to you, Angela.

'Is he getting it back?'

Sharp move.

'Well, that's the problem.'

'What do you mean?'

'He's starting to remember things, but in a confused manner, and very slowly. For example, he still can't work out why he was at the port when he was shot.'

'Poor man! So what do you talk about when you go to see him?'

'We talk about the little he can remember. His memory is functioning strangely. He can recall certain acts and situations, but has forgotten people's names and what they looked like.'

'What does Professor Bartolomeo say?'

'That it's going to take a long time.'

'Why did you have him moved to the attic?'

Bad move. A question you should never have asked, Angela.

'The commissioner asked for maximum protection. He's afraid someone may be trying to kill him.'

'But he can't remember anything!'

Excellent imitation of surprise.

'Yeah, but the problem is that the people who want to kill him don't know that.'

*

'What a beautiful place! Let's sit as close to the sea as possible.'

*

'I hope I'm not making too bad an impression on you.'

'Why do you say that?'

'I'm eating like a . . . But I just can't resist these anti-pasti.'

'I like women who like to eat. Shall I order another bottle?'

'Yes.'

*

'. . . to say nothing of what happens at the hospital! There used to be a doctor in A&E – fortunately he's gone now – who never gave me a moment's rest! Once he actually grabbed me without warning and wanted to make love in front of a dying patient . . . he said the situation excited him . . . Another time it was a recovering patient, a senior judge, who came up behind me as I was bending over and . . .'

*

'No, I didn't want to become a nurse, I wanted to get a degree in medicine, but then my father died, and his pension was barely enough for my mother and me, and so ... I already said it, didn't I? That sometimes we're forced to do things we don't want to do...'

'And have you had to do so often?'

Here's where we play rough, Angela.

'Had to do what?'

You know exactly what I mean. You're just stalling.

'Do things you didn't want to do.'

'Well, a few times, I suppose.'

'And have you ever had to do something against your will that in the end turned out to be pleasant?'

She didn't answer immediately. She realized that her answer would be important.

'Two or three times.'

On to the frontal attack.

'What about tonight?'

'I don't understand.'

Still stalling, Angela?

'Do you think it will turn out to have been pleasant?'

'Ask me again when it's over.'

She'd stopped laughing a while back. She continued:

'For now, though, everything's very pleasant indeed.'

Montalbano didn't say a word. She resumed.

'At any rate, nobody forced me to come out with you.'

That detail came slightly after the clock had run out.

*

'Shall we go?'

'Yes.'

'Shall I drive you back to Fiacca?'

'No.'

'Want to come to my place?'

'Yes.'

*

Montalbano started the car, but didn't drive off at once. He bent down as if he couldn't find something.

'What are you looking for?'

'I thought I'd...'

And they were off like a rocket, so fast that Angela was thrown back against her seat. In the rear-view mirror Montalbano saw the same metallic-finish car that had been following them since Fiacca hurry out of the car park in pursuit of them. Everything was falling into place. He started to slow down.

*

When driving past the Scala dei Turchi, he slowed down even more. By this point he was going barely twenty kilometres an hour, and every car that passed him had a few nasty things to say to him. The poor metallic car, with its powerful engine, must have been suffering terribly to have to keep behind him at that slow pace. Angela kept her head turned towards the sea and had stopped talking. Without warning Montalbano took his right hand off the steering wheel and laid it on the girl's left thigh. She didn't move. A few moments later the hand began to find its way between her legs, which Angela held tightly together. This time, too, she didn't breathe a word.

*

The moment they were inside the house, without a word Montalbano grabbed her by the waist with both hands and held her tightly against him. She didn't return his embrace, but let her body be pressed up against his.

When Montalbano sought out her lips, however, she jerked her head away.

'You don't want me to kiss you?'

'Yes, but not on the lips, please.'

'As you wish,' said Montalbano, starting to caress her breasts.

A moment later she asked:

'Could we have that whisky on the veranda?'

*

'I could sit here like this all night.'

She was on her second whisky. Sitting on the little

bench next to Montalbano, she was resting her head on his shoulder. The sky was crisp, polished clean, with more stars than the inspector ever saw except on rare occasions. A man in a hat walked slowly by along the water's edge. The two of them on the veranda were lit up as though on a stage, and yet the man didn't once turn his head to look at them.

You're an idiot, thought Montalbano. *Any normal passer-by would have looked.*

Was he the man driving the metallic car, or was he the one in the passenger's seat?

*

'Shall we go inside?'

'Could I have another whisky first?'

'A third glass? No. After all the wine you drank this evening, you'll get drunk.'

'What do you care?'

'I don't like making love to a drunken woman.'

Angela heaved a long sigh.

'All right, then, let's go inside.'

As they were getting up, a second man, without a hat, walked slowly past along the water's edge. My, what a lot of traffic there was on the beach tonight! Unlike the first one, however, this second man stopped and looked at them.

*

'This is the bedroom and the bathroom is there.'

He heard his mobile ring. He'd left it on the dining-room table.

'I'm going to answer that. Meanwhile, get undressed.'

He ran a hand lightly across her buttocks and went out.

*

He took the phone out onto the veranda before answering.

'Hello?'

'Fazio here, Chief.'

'At this hour?'

'You told me I could call no matter the hour.'

'I meant that for your sake. How come you're not asleep?'

'I can't fall asleep.'

'All right, what did you want to tell me?'

'I remembered Manzella's address. Via Bixio 22.'

'Thanks. Now try to get some sleep.'

The man on the beach hadn't moved and was still watching. Montalbano turned off the outdoor light and locked the French windows.

*

She hadn't got undressed. She merely sat at the edge of the bed, staring at her shoes.

'Would you prefer it if I undressed you myself?'

'You won't get upset if I tell you something?'

'Tell me.'

'I don't feel like it any more.'

'All right, then, I'll call a cab.'

She was disconcerted. She hadn't expected Montalbano to give up so quickly. Then she recovered and said: 'Couldn't I stay here a little while longer?'

She couldn't leave the house too early. To those waiting for her, it would mean she'd failed.

'Not here. Let's go back onto the veranda.'

'No. I feel cold outside.'

Sitting back down on the veranda, with that man still looking on, would mean that she hadn't accomplished anything.

'Listen, if we remain in the bedroom, the situation becomes harder and harder for me. You know what I mean?'

'Yes, but ...'

'We could make an agreement.'

'What do you mean?'

Come on, Montalbano, say it. The more vulgar you are, the more quickly she'll cave in.

'Just give me a blow job and I'll let you go.'

'No!'

'Would you please tell me why you've been so available? In fact, it was you who suggested we come to my place. And now, suddenly –' *even more vulgar, Montalbano –* 'and now you don't want to pull down your panties and spread your legs?'

She gave a start and put a hand on her left cheek, as if she'd been slapped.

'I don't feel like it any more, I've already told you.'

That's a lame excuse, Angela. But let's pretend it works.

'Listen, tell you what. I'll drive you back to Fiacca.'

'Right now?'

'Right now.'

'Couldn't we wait . . . an hour or so?'

'Just long enough so people will think we fucked?'

She shot to her feet.

'What are you talking about? *Who* will think?'

'Sit down.'

'No.'

He grabbed her by the arm and threw her down on the bed. She sat up, propping herself up with arms tensed and fists clenched.

'All right, this is where the gloves come off. Either you do what I say or I'll make you do it.'

'Please . . .'

'So you eat an' drink on me, an' now you say you don' feel like it no more? Thought you could fuck around wit' me, eh? I can play this old fart like a fiddle! Izzat whatchoo was thinkin', li'l bitch? Well, think again, 'cause I'm going to show you a thing or two!'

It wasn't so much the tone as the fact that he'd suddenly switched to dialect that seemed to terrify Angela. She looked at him as if seeing him for the first time.

'I thought you were … different.'

'You was wrong!'

In the twinkling of an eye, he furiously tore off his jacket and shirt and stood there barechested. He felt ridiculous, and probably looked it. Though ashamed of what he was doing, he had to continue the charade until she broke.

'Take off your blouse and bra.'

Still on the bed, she obeyed. For a second, Montalbano was spellbound by the sight of the girl's beautiful breasts.

'Now the rest, baby. C'mon!'

She stood up and, turning her back to him, took off her jeans.

For a second, Montalbano felt like St Anthony's twin brother.

'Now the panties.'

As soon as she took them off, Montalbano came up behind her and pulled down his zip, making as much noise as possible. Then he grabbed Angela by the hips.

'Bend over.'

She leaned against the back of a chair. His hands felt her shudder all over, and then she made a strange sound with her mouth, as if she'd been about to throw up and had strained to hold it in.

'Now get dressed,' he said, going and sitting on the edge of the bed.

As she was putting her jeans back on, the inspector saw her shoulders heave with sobs.

'Shall we drop the pretence now, and start talking seriously?'

'OK,' said Angela, sniffling like a little girl.

＊

'I already realized something wasn't right the first time we met. You made a big mistake.'

'What?'

'You asked me who I was looking for. And I replied that I wanted to visit a friend named Fazio who'd had an operation on his head. And you took me immediately to the fourth floor.'

'Where else was I supposed to take you? You know how hospitals are organized! Into wards. If you tell me your friend has had an operation on his head, I already know he's on the fourth floor, on Professor Bartolomeo's ward.'

'Of course. But how did you know he was in room six? You didn't ask anybody, you didn't look at any lists, you just took me straight to the right door. Do you want me to believe that you know the room numbers of all three hundred patients in the hospital?'

The girl bit her lip and said nothing.

They were sitting in the dining room, with the French windows closed.

Angela had gone to the bathroom and freshened herself up a little. And the inspector had put his shirt back on and then washed his own face in turn, as he had worked up a sweat during the performance.

'That same day, in the afternoon, I came back in my car, not the squad car I'd taken that morning. But you somehow knew I'd come in my own car. You alluded to this when we decided we'd come here to Vigàta. How did you happen to know? The visitors' car park is far from the hospital, you can't see it from the windows, and so someone must have told you. Isn't that right?'

Angela nodded yes.

'Another mistake: the elderly woman at the information desk didn't know that Fazio had been transferred. Whereas you, right before my eyes, went to ask her, then came back and took me straight to the lift that led to the attic. Therefore you already knew where Fazio had been taken and had just done a little playacting to make me think it was the old lady at the desk who'd told you. Isn't that right?'

'Yes.'

'One final mistake, much bigger than the rest. When I gave you the keys to my car, which I'd parked in a spot not easy to find, I gave you a registration number totally different from the real one. Still, when I came out later, there you were, in my car. Which meant that you knew my car so well from the description they'd given you, that you didn't even look at the licence plate.'

Montalbano poured himself a little whisky.

'Let me have a little of that too. I assure you I'm no longer in a state to get drunk,' said Angela.

The inspector gave her some.

'So how did they drag you into this mess?'

FOURTEEN

'You're a nice girl, I'm convinced. Want me to tell you how they did it?'

'You couldn't possibly know.'

'Lemme try an' guess. I'll ask you some questions and you just say yes or no. Did you lose your boyfriend when he died after being thrown into a well?'

She recoiled, eyes popping, turned pale, and muttered a few inaudible words the inspector couldn't grasp. The surprise had knocked the wind out of her. She tried again to speak.

'But ... how ... how did you ...'

'Don't worry about that, you've answered my question. So I'll go on. Then a friend of your boyfriend, somebody he always worked with, came to tell you what happened. A man with a big scar on his face. He told you that it was Fazio who killed him, and they wanted revenge. And that it was your duty to be part of the vendetta. All you

197

had to do was tell him what floor Fazio was on and what room he was in. And you went along with it.'

'But . . .'

'I know, you only told him the floor but not the room number. You had second thoughts, didn't you?'

'Yes, I didn't want . . . At first I was very angry and desperate, but then I thought that the poor man was only doing his duty.'

'Did you know that your boyfriend . . . What was his name?'

'Same as mine. Angelo. Angelo Sorrentino.'

'Did you know that he did the kind of things he did?'

'He never talked to me about it. But for the last few months I'd been suspecting something.'

'What's the name of the man with the scar?'

'Vittorio Carmona.'

'Is that him out there in the car?'

'Yes.'

'And who's the man with him?'

'I don't know.'

'So then you told Carmona you didn't want to have anything more to do with this business, and he black-mailed you. Is that right?'

'Yes, he told me he would write a letter saying it was me who let him into the hospital because I was Angelo's girlfriend. And if that wasn't enough to convince me, he would kill me.'

'What did he order you to do with me tonight?'

'He wanted me to sleep with you and make you talk.'

'What did they want to know?'

'What Fazio could remember, and whether he'd named any names.'

'But I'd already answered that question at the restaurant, so there was no need for you to sleep with me.'

'No, you're wrong, that wasn't the reason.'

'Why, then?'

'I suddenly thought of Angelo. And I couldn't do it. And then . . .'

'Then you realized you couldn't play Judas.'

She didn't reply. Her chin quivered.

'Is that all they wanted?'

'No.'

Now she was blushing red. She seemed offended.

'Come on, speak.'

'I'm too embarrassed.'

'Then I'll tell you myself. They wanted you to act in such a way that I would fall for you, become obsessed with your body, so that the relationship would continue for a while. That way they could know the police department's moves in advance.'

'I was supposed to become their whore, in every way. But what will I tell him now? Carmona'll kill me.'

'I'll tell you what to say to him. Now listen carefully.'

✽

He straggled into the station the next morning around nine, dead tired. He'd gone out of the house at four a.m. hand in hand with Angela, and then, for the benefit and enjoyment of any and all spectators and stalkers, they had given each other a long kiss, holding each other tight. Like two lovers for whom the night spent together hadn't sufficed. Feeling Angela's lips against his, however, Montalbano had realized that her kiss wasn't just playacting. There was also warm gratitude and affection in it. He'd felt his blood begin to boil and his head start to spin.

'Could I drive?' she asked.

The inspector gladly let her take the wheel. After that kiss, he'd remembered the sight of the girl's breasts and was in no condition to drive. He would have turned every straight stretch into a bend.

Angela drove well and fast. The metallic car was no longer following them. They must have left after a while, convinced that he and Angela were rolling around in bed. Still, it took the girl an hour and fifteen minutes to get to Fiacca.

On the return drive, however, it took the inspector an hour and fifty. Back in Marinella, he took a shower that used up nearly all the water, then drank five cups of coffee in a row.

He hadn't even finished parking when he heard Catarella's voice cry out in distress.

'Ahh, Chief, Chief! Ahh, Chief!' he yelled, running towards the car.

It had to be something serious. Montalbano didn't even bother getting out of the car.

'Jeez, iss so long I bin tryin' a call yiz, Chief! But you got yer home phone unplagged an' yer mobble phone turned of'

'All right, what happened?'

'A lady was killed!'

'Is Inspector Augello at the scene?'

'Yessir, Chief. 'e tol' me hisself, poissonally in poisson, a tell yiz poissonally in poisson 'atta minnit ya got in y'gotta call 'im emergently! 'Ass what 'e tol' me a tell yiz.'

'Give me the address.'

Catarella searched his pockets. 'I writ it onna piss a paper I can't find. Ah, 'ere it is! But iss not too ligible. Sumpin' like nummer thirteen, Via della Forchella or Forchetta.'

It had to be Via della Forcella.

'I'm going to go there right . . .'

The inspector suddenly stopped. He'd just remembered who lived on that street.

✳

There was pandemonium when he got there. TV cameras, journalists, and some thirty people gathered outside the door, kept at bay by the curses and expletives of two municipal police officers. Every balcony of the building was crammed full of people looking on in excitement. He got out of the car and made his way through the crowd by dint of pushing and swearing. A newsman grabbed him by the arm.

'Tell us please what you think of all this!'

'What do *you* think of it?'

The man was thrown off balance, allowing Montalbano to go on. The body lay in the main entrance, half inside, half outside, feet taking in the fresh air, partially covered by a bloody sheet. Galluzzo came running up to the inspector.

'The victim was the concierge of the building. Fifty-four years old, named Matilde Verruso.'

'How was she killed?'

'When she went to open the front door early this morning, she was shot by somebody inside a car, which then sped off.'

'Any witnesses?'

'Someone on the third floor. He was sitting looking out of the window when—'

'I'd like to question him later. Where's Augello?'

'Inside.'

The inspector took two steps and turned back.

'But if she was shot early this morning, why's the body still here?'

'Because at almost exactly the same moment they killed this poor woman, the Mayor of Gallotta was murdered, and everybody rushed there first. They should all be here in forty-five minutes or so.'

Right. Politics takes priority. He went inside the porter's lodge and heard somebody snoring. 'Who's that sleeping?' he asked Mimì.

'The husband. He's stinking drunk.'

'Listen, do you know where I might find the key to Manzella's flat?'

'There's no point in going there. I've already checked it out myself. I had the same idea as you.'

'And?'

'The telescope you mentioned to me is gone, and so are the binoculars. They took 'em.'

'When?'

'What do you mean?'

'Mimì, think for a second. If the men who shot her drove away immediately, they couldn't have taken the telescope and binoculars. Not even after committing the murder. They disappeared before the murder. Is that clear to you?'

'Perfectly.'

'I want to talk to that witness.'

'Mr Catalfamo? Third floor, number twelve. But basically, he didn't see anything.'

'I want to talk to him anyway.'

*

Montalbano had to ring the doorbell a long time. Apparently Mr Catalfamo was out on the balcony and couldn't hear it. At last he decided to come in and answer the door. A substantial cloud of garlic smell took advantage of the situation to waft out of the apartment.

'I'm Inspector Montalbano, police.'

'And I'm Eugenio Catalfamo, retired, widower, no children, seventy-eight years old. Come in, come in.'

'No, thank you, Mr Catalfamo, I only need to ask you a question.'

'Please come in just the same.'

The poor man wanted someone to talk to. But how long would Montalbano be able to hold his breath?

'All right, thanks.'

He went in. The apartment was exactly the same as Manzella's. There were two chairs around a small table.

Catalfamo pulled one out for him.

'Please make yourself comfortable. Can I get you anything?'

'No, thanks.'

The inspector couldn't stand it. He pulled a handkerchief out of his pocket and put it over his nose.

'I'm sorry, but I have a bad cold. I only wanted to know if you got a good look at what happened.'

'I got good eyes.'

'I'm glad. Did you see the car the gunman fired from?'

'Of course I saw it! It arrived less than a minute before poor Signura Matilde reopened the front door. She didn't even have time to make a peep, poor thing! They just fired and drove away!'

Why would Signora Matilde have wanted to make a peep? 'Do you remember the registration number?'

'I didn't pay any attention.'

'How about the colour?'

'Metallic blue. Big car.'

He'd expected that reply. After finishing their guard duty in Marinella, Vittorio Carmona and his associate had left at the crack of dawn to attend to a little early morning business. But something the pensioner had said didn't quite add up.

'I'm sorry, Mr Catalfamo, you said something about the concierge and the open door that I didn't quite get.'

'I only sleep three hours a night, Inspector.'

'I'm sorry. It happens to the best of us.'

'If it's nice outside, I go out on the balcony at four in the morning.'

'Did you see anything this morning?'

'This morning, just before five, a little van came up and stopped in front of the main door. A man got out and rang the buzzer. I's leaning way out to get a good look at 'im. I wanted to see whose number he'd buzzed. A minute later the front door opened an' Signura Matilde came out an' started talking to him. As they was talkin' Mr Di Mattia came out. He works in Ravanusa, so he's gotta leave early. Then the man went inside and came back out with a big telescope that he put in his van. Signura Matilde also gave him a package. The guy took it, drove away, an' the signura closed the door again.'

'What floor does Mr Di Mattia live on?'

'Fourth floor. I'm sure his wife's there.'

*

'Mrs Di Mattia?'

'Yes?'

'I'm Inspector Montalbano, police.'

'Please come in. My husband's not here. He works in—'

'Ravanusa, I know. Does your husband have a mobile phone?'

'Yes, sir.'

'Could you give me the number?'

*

He went back down to the porter's lodge. The sleeping man was snoring even louder. Mimì was sitting at a small table with some papers scattered in front of him.

'I've had a look at these and found something interesting.'

'What?'

'That just four days ago, the concierge deposited five thousand euros in the bank. Doesn't that seem strange?'

'Listen, Mimì, there are a number of new developments we need to talk about. You wait here for the prosecutor, coroner, Forensics, and the rest of those clowns, and I'll see you later at the station.'

'Can't you give me a hint of these new developments?'

'It'd be better when we had a little time.'

'And where are you going now?'

'I'm not going to tell you, or you'll get envious. What time did you tell Rizzica to come in?'

'I told him to come around noon, but he said he'd be busy all morning. He'll be there around four in the afternoon.'

*

The inspector made his way through the crowd, cursing the saints. A TV reporter tried to buttonhole him, but he told him to go to hell, then got in his car and drove off. Turning down a narrow, deserted side street, he pulled out his mobile phone and dialled Di Mattia's number.

'Mr Di Mattia? Inspector Montalbano here, police.'

'What is it, Inspector?'

'Are you aware that the concierge of your building has been murdered?'

'Yes, my wife called and told me. And just now she called back to tell me she gave you my mobile-phone number.'

'Listen, Mr Catalfamo told me you went out this morning around five.'

'As always.'

'When you went downstairs, was the front door to the building open or closed?'

'It was closed, but poor Signora Matilde was about to open it, because someone had just buzzed outside.'

'Did you notice anything strange?'

'Well, *strange*, no, not really. Signora Matilde had just put a large telescope in the entrance to be taken away.'

'Did she say whose it was?'

'I asked her myself. She said it belonged to Mr Manzella, who'd called her the day before and said he would send a small van to come and pick it up. And, in fact, when I went out, I stopped for a second to retie my shoelace and saw Signora Matilde talking to the driver. But . . .'

'But what?'

'Isn't five o'clock in the morning a little early to come and get a telescope?'

Clever man, Mr Di Mattia.

*

Now he had to go to Manzella's other residence. But he'd already forgotten the address Fazio had given him. The only thing was to call him.

'Fazio? Montalbano here.'

'I recognized you, Chief.'

'How are you?'

'I'm well.'

'Any news?'

'This morning one of our police doctors came and then went off to talk to Professor Bartolomeo.'

'What did they decide?'

'That an ambulance is going to come this evening around six and take me to Palermo.'

'Why Palermo?'

'Because he says I have to remain under strict surveillance for another three or four days. Then I can leave. But our doctor says I need a good twenty days at the very least to fully recover.'

'So much the better for you.'

'I'm going to spend my convalescence in Vigàta, Chief.'

'So? That way I can come and see you every so often.'

'Every so often? I'm going to come to the station every day, just like I was on the job.'

Montalbano said nothing. Without Fazio around, he felt as if one of his arms had been cut off.

'I'm sorry I don't have the time to come and say hello.'

'Listen, Chief, since my wife's coming to see me in Palermo tomorrow morning, she'll bring your gun back to you this evening at the station.'

'All right. Well, goodbye then. Ah, I almost forgot! Could you tell me that address Manzella gave you again?'

'Of course. Via Bixio 22.'

'Thanks, Fazio. Take care, and I'll see you soon.'

*

He decided to make another call immediately. He glanced at his watch: ten thirty.

Too bad if he woke her up.

'Hello, Angela. Montalbano here.'

'Hello, Salvo.'

She sounded still asleep.

'Did I wake you up?'

'No, I just got up, but I haven't had my coffee yet.'

'Then I'll let you go. I just wanted to know whether your friend had called yet to find out what had happened between us and what I told you.'

'Not yet. But I'm sure he'll be calling soon.'

'Listen, I wanted to let you know that Fazio's going to be picked up by ambulance this evening around six and taken to Palermo.'

'Am I supposed to tell them that, too?'

'Yes. It's why I called you.'

'What exactly do you want me to say?'

'Tell them I called to hear your voice and find out if you'd had a good sleep, things like that, and in the course of the conversation I mentioned the ambulance. That should work, no?'

'Yes, I think so. Listen, since I get off work at ten tonight, I was thinking it'll be too late to go out to eat at a restaurant.'

'I'll have something made here.'

'Then I'll just come to your place in my car. And stay until four.'

'All right.'

And while he was at it . . .

*

'Adelì? Montalbano here.'

'Wha' izzit, Isspector?'

'Could you please change the sheets on my bed? And then why don't you go ahead and set up the sofa with a mattress and three chairs the way you do? And cook me something nice for this evening, and make a lot of it.'

*

And while he was still at it . . .

'Catarella? Montalbano here.'

'Yessir, Chief.'

'I need you to search through the files for two men who probably have records.'

'Jess a sec, Chief, whiles I git a pin and paper. Whass the names?'

'The first is Angelo Sorrentino. Write it down correctly. Did you write it?'

'Yeah.'

'Repeat it for me.'

'Ponentino.'

'No, not Ponentino! Fuck! Sorrentino. Like someone who was born in Sorrento. Don't you know the song?'

'Chief, if I sing the song, i' comes out Surrientino.'

Finally, after the inspector had cursed a number of saints, Catarella got it right.

'An' whattabout th'other one, Chief?'

'His name's Vittorio Carmona. Did you get that?'

'Cammona, Chief.'

'No, not Cammona, but Carmona, with an *r*!'

'An' wha'd I say? I said Cammona wit' an *r*!'

'Listen, when you find them, don't put the files on my desk. Give them to me personally in person when I get back.'

FIFTEEN

He had utterly no idea where Via Bixio was. And he didn't
dare ask Catarella, who would surely have thought he'd
said Via Piscio. He had a map of Vigàta that he kept with
him in the car. He took it out of the glove compartment
and studied it. The index of street names said it was in
box C4. It was like playing Battleships. Naturally, and
predictably, a piece of the map had been torn away, the
very part that contained box C4. But the inspector managed
to work out that Via Bixio was past San Giusippuzzo, in
a district that was almost open country.

It took him about half an hour to get there. Number
22 Via Bixio, which at one point turned into a country
lane, was a tiny bungalow surrounded by what must have
once been a cross between an orchard and a kitchen garden
but was now in a state of total abandon. In front was a
wrought-iron gate, left open. Montalbano went in and
down the little path to the house. The door was locked,
and the windows too. There was a doorbell, which he rang

and rang, but nobody came. Seeing that the closest house was a good fifty yards away and there wasn't a single car to be seen anywhere all the way to the horizon, he pulled out of his jacket pocket a special set of keys a burglar friend of his had given to him. On his fourth try, the door came open, and he leapt backwards, just as he had done when Mr Catalfamo had opened the door. But this time it wasn't garlic he smelled. It was the bittersweet and thoroughly unpleasant odour of blood, which he had smelled so many times before. He slipped inside and closed the door behind him, holding his breath. He felt the wall, searching for the light switch, found it, and flipped it on. He was in a living room whose furniture had all been pushed up against the walls. Alone in the middle of the room was a wicker chair, completely darkened with dried blood. Blood had also been spattered all over the walls, furniture, and floor. A real slaughter. The chair stood at the centre of a broad circle of brown blood, as if someone had gone round and round it . . .

Suddenly Montalbano understood what they had done in that room. For a second he saw the scene with his own eyes, and an irrational, unbearable fear came over him. Instinctively, he took a deep breath, and the terrible smell triggered a violent wave of nausea. He stepped back, opened the door, closed it, got back in the car, and left. But after a minute or two he had to stop. He got out and vomited.

*

'Ahh, Chief! I gots the files 'ere y'axed me 'bout fer Cammona wit' a *r* an' Ponentino whose rill name's Sorrentino. Ah, an' afore I ferget, Mr Gargiuto called. 'E says as how as soon as you's onna premises a call.'

'Cat, I didn't understand a word you said. Who's supposed to call, me or Gargiuto?'

'Youse, Chief.'

'But if I don't even know who this Gargiuto is, how am I supposed to call him?'

'You don' know 'im, Chief? You rilly mean 'at?' Catarella asked, looking at him in amazement.

'Never heard of him.'

'Whattya mean, Chief? Y'tol' me 'e's asposta, 'e meanin' Gargiuto, 'e's asposta give yiz, yiz bein' youse, Chief, a answer 'bout you givin' 'im a litter wroten in so much as . . .'

Gargiulo of Forensics!

'I got it, I got it. Listen, is Inspector Augello in?'

''E jess call sayin' as how 'e's going to be on 'is way in a half hour.'

'As soon as you see him, tell him to come to my office.'

*

'What can you tell me, Gargiù?'

'I can give you a quick answer right away, Inspector. For a more thorough analysis I'm going to need three or four days.'

'Just give me the quick answer for now.'

'The handwriting's not natural.'

'You mean it's faked?'

'Absolutely not. I mean it's purposely made to look the way it does.'

'By whom?'

'By whoever wrote it.'

'Let me get this straight, Gargiù. The person writing the letter didn't like the handwriting mother nature gave him, and so he forced himself to write differently?'

'Something like that. So the author of the letter, a man—'

'Are you sure of that?'

'If I tell you this G is a man, he's a man, believe me. But a man who's forcing himself to write with feminine handwriting. Do you understand?'

'Of course.'

'Now, in three or four days, when—'

'Listen, Gargiù, don't bother. You've already told me enough. Thanks, I really appreciate it, and please send the letter back to me right away.'

'I'll have an officer run it over to you right now.'

*

'So, what's the news?' Augello asked, coming in after Montalbano had been signing papers for a good half an hour.

'I'll tell you in a minute. So, how'd it go yesterday with Mrs Manzella?'

'She identified the body.'

'How did she react to the news?'

'Let's just say she was mildly displeased.'

'Didn't I tell you the news wouldn't be quite so bad for her? She's not only going to inherit, she's going to get married straightaway.'

'So, what's the news?' Augello repeated.

'The first thing is that you should postpone Rizzica's visit till tomorrow.'

'Why?'

'Because this afternoon, no later than five, you have to be at Fiacca Hospital, where Fazio's staying. I want you to bring Gallo and Galluzzo with you, and make sure you're well armed.'

'What do you want us to do?'

'Around six an ambulance is going to come and get Fazio and take him to Palermo.'

'So?'

'You three are going to be his escort. But discreetly. Don't attract any attention. I want you to take your own car. If they still want to eliminate him, this is their last chance.'

'But do you seriously believe—'

'Yes, Mimì, I seriously do. They already proved it a second time at the hospital.'

'And how would they do it this time?'

'I can tell you, with ninety per cent certainty, that there'll be a big metallic-blue car following the ambulance. If you see it, beware! It's them. They might even try to cause an accident, and in the confusion try to kill Fazio. And I'll tell you something else: it's the same car from which the gunmen shot the concierge this morning.'

'Fuck! And how do you know about this car?'

Now came the hard part. It was absolutely imperative that he keep Angela out of the picture. She had to remain completely invisible. If he compromised her in any way at all, the girl could consider herself dead.

'I happened to talk to the nurse who chased away the man who had slipped onto Fazio's ward. She gave such a good description of him to Fiacca's Chief Inspector Caputo that he was able to identify him in no time.'

'So who is he?'

'His name is Vittorio Carmona. Fugitive, wanted for three murders. A member of the Sinagra family. Have a look at his file.'

He pulled it out of a drawer. The other file, Sorrentino's, he'd hidden at the bottom, under a stack of papers. No one must see it. He would stick it in his pocket before leaving and then burn it at home.

'Nice, honest-looking face,' commented Augello, giving the file back to him. Then he asked: 'So how did you know about the car?'

'I talked to the employee at the hospital car park, you

THE DANCE OF THE SEAGULL

know, the man at the gate. Inspector Caputo hadn't got round to it,' he said, in the heartfelt hope that Mimì wouldn't talk to either the employee or Inspector Caputo.

'Are we going to talk about the concierge?' Mimì asked.

'You have any ideas about her?'

'Yup.'

'Let's hear them.'

'When Manzella left the telescope there, the concierge must have become curious. So one night she got up and looked at it. And she must have seen something that put her in a position to blackmail someone. And whoever it was paid up at once, just to keep things quiet. Then they went into Manzella's flat and took the binoculars and telescope, and as soon as it was daylight, they killed her.'

'Wrong.'

'Where?'

'The second part.'

'Explain.'

'Mimì, I've got two witnesses who can testify that it was Signora Matilde herself, the concierge, who gave the telescope and binoculars to a man who came around five thirty in the morning, in a van.'

'Then that changes every—'

'And there's more. Signora Matilde told one of the witnesses that Manzella had called her the day before, and she was having the stuff sent to his new address.'

'Imagine that! He'd been already dead for days!'

'So the question is this: if she wasn't having the stuff sent to its rightful owner, who was she sending it to? Think about it.'

Mimì thought about it for a minute and then came to the logical conclusion.

'To whoever she was blackmailing!'

'See? You can be pretty good when you put your mind to it!'

'But by doing that, she got rid of the only potential evidence she had!'

'How much did she have in the bank, Mimì?'

'Five thousand euros.'

'Did you search her place?'

'No! Why would I do that?'

'Because surely there must be some more money stashed away somewhere, in a bag or envelope or something. They made a deal, money for telescope and binoculars. Paid in advance. What's the situation like down there?'

'The porter's gone off to get drunk again, and the flat's been sealed off.'

'Excellent. Later, in due course, we'll go and have a look.'

'So in your opinion, after the second cash instalment in exchange for the binoculars and telescope, the game was over?'

'At least that's what they wanted her to believe. And

THE DANCE OF THE SEAGULL

then they shot her a few hours later. And that's the real problem.'

'I don't understand.'

'Let's recapitulate, that'll help you to understand. The whole story begins with a man named Manzella who wants to report some smuggling to his friend Fazio. Fazio doesn't mention it to us, but the same day Fazio disappears, Mr Rizzica comes and tells us that he's suspicious of the crew of one of his trawlers and thinks they might be using the boat for drug trafficking. Notice the difference?'

'You mean the coincidence?'

'Mimì, I speak good Italian because I read books. You, on the other hand, are as ignorant as a sheep and confuse words. I said difference, not coincidence.'

'And what is this thing, whatever it is?'

'You see? Is that any way to express yourself? You've become an honorary Catarellian. The difference lies in the fact that Manzella talked about smuggling, whereas Rizzica came to report drug trafficking.'

'What kind of difference is that? Don't we say drug smuggling?'

'Perhaps. But in common speech we use the word trafficking. Nobody ever says drug smuggling.'

'What is this, school?'

'No. If it were, I would have already failed you. I'm just pointing out an important distinction for you.

Smuggling can involve just about anything: weapons, cigarettes, medicines, nuclear-bomb materials.'

'But is Fazio so sure Manzella said smuggling?'

'Absolutely certain. And it makes sense to me.'

'Why?'

'Let's resume our recapitulation, so you can understand, too. Manzella waffles for a few days, then makes an appointment to meet Fazio at the port. Fazio doesn't realize it's a trap, because Manzella's already been murdered. So he goes to the meeting. He gets shot and wounded, and his aggressors decide to finish him off far outside town, at the three wells. But then the unexpected happens: Fazio manages to break free and pushes one of them into the well.'

'Who hasn't been identified yet.'

'Right.'

A solemn fib, since all he had to do was pull the file out of the drawer, and Mimì would have known the man's first and last names. The problem was that Montalbano couldn't do or say anything, or Angela was screwed.

'But,' the inspector continued, 'we do know that one of the two men was our same Vittorio Carmona, since Fazio identified him immediately when I described him for him.'

'And then they killed the concierge.'

'Exactly. Two killings – actually three, except that Fazio did it in self-defence – and an attempted murder that they're going to try to finish, I'm sure of it. Don't you think that's a lot?'

'A lot of what?'

'A lot of dead people, Mimì. And that's the point. Too many killings for a simple case of drug trafficking. We're not in Bolivia.'

'And so?'

'And so there's probably something really big at the bottom of all this.'

'If only we could know how Manzella found out about the whole thing and why he wanted to tell Fazio about it . . .' Augello started saying.

'Wait a minute,' said Montalbano.

He picked up the phone.

'Catarella, has Forensics sent anything over to me?'

'Yessir, Chief. Jess right now. A litter.'

'Bring it to me, would you?'

As soon as Catarella brought it, Mountalbano opened the envelope and handed the letter to Mimì.

'Is this written by a man or a woman?' asked Augello after reading it.

'I had the same question. So I asked Gargiulo to have a look at it, and he said it was definitely written by a man who wants to pass for a woman.'

'A transvestite? Transsexual?'

'Perhaps. Here, read this too.'

He opened the drawer, took out the letter from

Manzella's friend, the one with the photograph of the sailor, and handed it to him.

'There we are,' was Mimì's only comment.

'In my opinion,' said the inspector, 'our friend Manzella, married and the father of an only son, at a certain point in his life discovered a completely different world. And he realized he was made for that world. It's his own business and should be of no concern to us.'

'Relatively speaking,' said Mimì.

'Why do you say that?'

'Because just the other day Beba pointed out to me that if we were all like them, we would betray our purpose on earth, which is to procreate.'

'Whoever told you that's our purpose in life? The Lord God himself, poissonally in poisson? Tell me the truth: before you got married, when you were fucking everything that moved, didn't you do everything within your power not to procreate? The human race could have become extinct for all you cared!'

'What's that got to do with it?'

'Let's just drop the subject, Mimì, it's better that way. So, to continue. On a dark day for him, Manzella meets G. It's love at first sight, if you'll pardon the cliché and the pain it may cause you, great converted procreator that you are. They get together often, until Manzella discovers by chance, or perhaps because G tells him, that his friend is involved in some shady stuff. But he doesn't want to lose him, and so he keeps his mouth shut. Until one day somebody tells him that G is cheating on him. And so he decides to take revenge and tells Fazio what's going on. But then he has second thoughts and backtracks. He has his ups and downs. And ends up letting G know his intentions. G warns whoever he needs to warn, and they silence him. Make sense to you?'

'It's a plausible hypothesis,' said Augello.

'It's the only one possible,' said Montalbano, standing up. 'But there's no proof.'

'Where are you going?'

'To eat. But take care, Mimì. When you're tailing the ambulance, ring me every fifteen minutes on the mobile. Don't forget that you can arrest Carmona whenever you like, since he's a murderer and a fugitive from justice. But don't forget that he's also dangerous and won't hesitate for a second to start shooting. And when he shoots, it's not just to make noise.'

'All right then, if I can, I'll let you listen to the shooting over the phone, to help pass the time,' said Mimì.

*

Actually the inspector had no intention whatsoever of going to eat. In fact, since what he had to do was something that didn't appeal to him at all, his stomach felt so tight that not even a bread crumb could have passed his lips.

He was also certain that if he did eat, he wouldn't be able to do what he had to do afterwards.

There are things that cannot be faced on a full stomach. He knew this from experience.

One time, when he'd had to watch Pasquano working on the corpse of a ten-year-old girl just after he'd finished eating, he spent a good fifteen minutes in the car park doubled over, throwing up his soul. It wasn't what Pasquano was doing, which he was obliged to watch, that had made him sick. No, it was the way the doctor was cataloguing out loud the wounds the little girl had suffered (*deep cut in the left calf inflicted by the same blade that . . . broad laceration in the groin area probably produced by an object . . .*) and he had imagined — no, he had seen, actually seen, the murder unfold, as if it was taking place right before his eyes, and he'd felt suffocated by the ferocity, the violence, the horrific bestiality . . .

Passing Catarella, he said goodbye and repeated the fib he'd told Augello.

'I'm going to eat, but I'll take my mobile phone, so you can call me at any time.'

He went out, took three steps, then returned.

'Did Fazio's wife bring back my gun?'

Catarella was astonished. 'Your gun? Signura Fazio? She's got a licence?'

'I don't think so.'

'An' she walks aroun' wit a gun in her poisse?'

'C'mon, Cat, no need to drag things out, I understand, she hasn't brought it in yet. But she will, and when she does, I want you to take it and give it to me when I return.'

What had made him think about the gun? Where he was going, it was ninety-nine per cent certain he wouldn't need it. And yet...

He got into his car and set off for Via Bixio.

Another question: why hadn't he told Mimì Augello he'd found out the address of Manzella's last place of residence and had even gone there?

It wasn't something he needed to keep hidden so as not to compromise Angela. The girl had nothing to do with it. Fazio had told him the address as soon as it had come back to him. And so?

The reason was so simple that he found it right away.

If he'd told Mimì he'd been to Manzella's place, Mimì would have asked him what he'd found there, and he would have had to say, yes, he'd gone inside but immediately run away.

He could imagine the look of astonishment on Mimì's face.

'You ran away?! Why'd you do that?'

And he would have to tell him he got scared.

'You? Scared? Of what?'

'Nothing concrete, Mimì. Let's just say I was metaphysically disconcerted.'

'Metaphysically what? What are you talking about?'

No, Augello would have thought he was going crazy.

Nor could he lie again and tell him he'd found out from Fazio where Manzella's last place of residence was but hadn't gone there yet because he wanted Mimì to go there with him. Augello knew him too well not to realize that the inspector would never have been able to resist the curiosity and would have rushed there at once, not giving a flying fuck about telling him or not.

So how was he going to get out of this?

Here's how: he would tell Mimì that Fazio had rung him from the mobile phone with the address as he was leaving the hospital or along the road to Palermo, because it hadn't come back to him until then, and he couldn't tell him because he was part of Fazio's escort.

Meanwhile he'd arrived in front of Manzella's house.

SIXTEEN

He stopped and got out. The road seemed even more deserted than before, if that was possible. No one would notice him. And even if, in passing by, somebody saw some movement, they would have no reason to become suspicious, since the local television stations hadn't announced that the corpse found in the well had been identified as Manzella.

The inspector didn't go through the gate immediately, but stopped outside the house, establishing the exact location of the windows and memorizing the path he would have to take to reach them from the living room.

Then he made up his mind. He went down the little lane, opened the door with his false key, went in, closed it behind him, and without turning on the lights, without breathing, proceeded, hand in front of him in the pitch darkness, straight to the first window and threw open the shutters. He stuck his head out and breathed deeply and long. The air was humid, the sky overcast. He was panting hard, as if after a long swim. Then he closed his eyes, turned around, and again holding his breath, went and opened the second window. Sticking his head out, he caught his breath again.

A light wind had started blowing, and the weather had suddenly changed, though it had been in a variable mood since morning. At any rate the wind helped. It would help the air flow between the two windows and get rid of the smell of blood. Still at the window, he lit a cigarette and smoked it calmly to the end. When he'd finished, he put the butt in his pocket. One never knew. The gentlemen of Forensics might find it, and might even have it tested for DNA. And Arquà would have to reach the logical and inevitable conclusion that the person who'd killed Manzella was none other than him, in a fit of jealousy over a transvestite.

At last he felt ready to turn around and look into the living room.

But since he immediately saw, on the right, a staircase leading to the first floor, he decided to go and check the rooms upstairs.

He went up and reached a tiny landing with three rooms with their doors wide open. He turned on the landing light. It was enough to allow him to see, without moving, but only turning his head, that the first door, the one right in front of him, gave onto a master bedroom, the second to a bathroom, and the third to another, smaller bedroom with a single bed, clearly for guests.

He started with the last, going in and turning the light on. There was only a mattress and pillow on the bed, no sheets or blankets. A bedside table with a lamp, two chairs, a small wardrobe. He opened it. There were sheets, a pillowcase, and two woollen blankets, all folded, and nothing else. On the night he was murdered, Manzella could not have had a guest sleeping in that room.

The bathroom, on the other hand, was a shambles. Four blood-stained towels thrown helter-skelter on the floor, traces of blood on the sink, and even a bloody handprint on the wall of the shower stall. It was clear: Carmona and Sorrentino, to work Manzella over with the blades and tips of their knives, had taken their clothes off and then, after getting covered with blood, had showered and put their clothes back on. To cleanse themselves for human society as humans and not as the beasts they were.

He moved on to the master bedroom. And it became immediately clear to the inspector that Pasquano had been right when he said that the poor man had been surprised by the two killers while sleeping naked in bed. In fact, on a chair were a pair of trousers, folded up, a jacket, a shirt, and even a tie. Under the chair were a pair of shoes with the socks rolled up inside.

Manzella did not, however, spend the last night of his life alone, or at least not all of it. The pillows were both still indented from where the heads had lain, and the top sheet was dangling, half on the floor, all twisted up, while the bottom sheet had come partly off, exposing the mattress.

Poor old Manzella was a man of fiery passion, as the concierge had said.

There was no sign of the clothes of the person who had slept with him, and there was no blanket, either. It must have been the one they'd used to roll up the body and throw it into the well.

Montalbano approached the chair with the clothes on it and took a wallet out of the inside pocket of the jacket. Five hundred euros in fifty-euro notes, ID card, debit card issued by the Banca dell'Isola, credit card from the same bank, which must have been the one where Manzella kept his money. And nothing else. The inspector opened the drawer in the bedside table: empty. There wasn't a single sheet of paper in the bedroom. The killers had taken everything, just to be safe.

But what had actually happened in there?

Montalbano had no trouble imagining it. So, after writing the letter that Manzella never received because he'd moved out, G managed one way or another to meet him again and renew the relationship that Manzella had tried to break off.

G had to do this, because, having confessed that he'd spoken to his lover about the smuggling, and that the latter intended to inform the police, the smugglers let him live, on condition that he assisted them in the murder of

Manzella. If he wouldn't or couldn't lead them to him, they would kill G.

And so he does and says what he has to do and say, and succeeds in getting invited a first time to the house in Via Bixio. As they say in novels about love — the kind that book reviewers like so much — the old flame was rekindled. The two make love, and G promises to come back the following night.

Which he does, and when Manzella falls asleep, exhausted, G picks up his clothes, goes downstairs very quietly, opens the door, lets in Carmona and Sorrentino, whom he'd alerted beforehand, and leaves. He's done what he was supposed to do, and so they let him go free.

Could I make a parenthetical comment here? the inspector asked himself.

Permission granted, he commented:

There are two possibilities: either G is a fool, believes the promise, and remains in Vigàta — and in this case we'll soon find his bullet-riddled body abandoned somewhere — or else he's shrewd and by now has already flown to northern Greenland, an area that, as everybody knows, has not yet been penetrated by the Sicilian Mafia, since it's too cold up there.

End of parenthesis.

Carmona and Sorrentino go upstairs, wake Manzella up, and force him downstairs, naked as the day he was born. They don't even let him put on his slippers, which were still on the floor beside the bed.

And this meant that the moment had come, willy-nilly, for Montalbano, too, to go into the living room.

He stopped on the landing at the top of the stairs, counting the steps. There were sixteen.

He wished he had his pistol in his hand. Even though he knew it would have been useless, since there was nothing to shoot at. He felt the hair on his arms stand on end, as when one brushes past a television set that has just been turned off, no matter how hard he tried to control himself and kept repeating in his mind that there was nobody waiting for him in the living room . . .

Of course there was nobody! Nobody in flesh and blood, that is. What was this nonsense, anyway? What was he afraid of, a ghost? A shade? So he was starting to believe in ghosts at age fifty-seven and counting?

He descended two stairs.

A shutter slammed hard, and he jumped in the air like a startled cat, so spooked he nearly lost his grip of the banister.

The wind had picked up.

With eyes closed, he dashed down the next four stairs. But then he suddenly lost heart and descended two more stairs, gripping the banister tightly and sliding his foot until it found emptiness, then slowly raising his leg and setting the sole of his shoe down lightly on the step below, exactly like someone partly or totally blind.

But what the hell was all this tension? He'd never felt

this way before. Was it some sort of nasty joke of old age?

This time the shutters of the living-room windows slammed with a loud thud and closed simultaneously. Now the room downstairs was in darkness again.

How was that possible? the inspector wondered. If the wind was blowing from one direction, how could both windows slam shut at the same time?

He suddenly understood that there actually *was* someone waiting for him in the living room.

Someone who had the same body and face as him, and who had the same name: Salvo Montalbano. He himself was the invisible enemy he would have to face. The enemy who would force him to relive what had happened in that room, down to the smallest details . . .

Relive? Wrong word. He hadn't witnessed Manzella's slow, painful death. How, then, could he relive it? And, anyway, after all the murders of which he'd seen so many vestiges that it was sometimes more upsetting than if he'd witnessed the murders themselves, why did this one have such a strong effect on him?

He would never get out of this situation unless he saw it through to the end, of that he was immediately certain.

And for this reason, he began descending the remaining stairs with as decisive a step as he could muster.

He stopped again at the bottom of the staircase.

The room was not completely in darkness. The shutters

were closed, but through the slats filtered blades of grey light that cast the trembling shadows of the windblown leaves on the trees outside. He wanted neither to reopen the shutters nor to light the lamps, but only to stand still for a moment until his eyes slowly adjusted.

To make space for the show they were about to direct, Carmona and Sorrentino had pushed all the furniture up against the wall. A table that had once had a small ceramic fruit bowl on it, which was now on the floor, shattered. Three chairs. A sofa. A small dining table, a sideboard with dishes and glasses. A television set.

There were two milky white things on the floor, near the dining table, which he couldn't quite identify.

It couldn't be. He realized immediately what they were but refused to believe it. He looked at them more closely, needing to convince himself that he'd seen correctly, as the disorder in the pit of his stomach, a knot of dense liquid, bitter and burning, began to rise into his throat, bringing tears to his eyes.

He started looking around the chair in the middle of the room and the dark circle of blood surrounding it.

The floor was made of terracotta, and he noticed that one tile, right in front of the chair, had been freshly splintered. If he'd had a knife handy, he could easily have extracted the bullet that, after passing through Manzella's foot, had shattered the tile and buried itself in the ground.

Mimì was right.

They'd taken him out of bed and down the stairs,

moved the furniture out of the way except for the chair in the middle of the room, sat him down . . . No, first they . . . *Go on, get it out, it's better that way.*

They started asking him – surely slapping him around, and kicking and punching – what he'd told Fazio . . .

But he could only give them one answer: that he'd only hinted at the matter with Fazio, and hadn't named any names . . . And they didn't believe him, and decided to get more serious.

'You used to be a ballet dancer, right?'

'Yes.'

'So dance, then.'

And one of them shot him in the foot. Then they forced him to stand up on one leg, the one with the uninjured foot, and made him dance around the chair.

'C'mon, dance, dance, an' don' make any noise.'

And so Manzella hopped around the chair on one foot, naked, at once comical and terrifying, emitting desperate cries that no one could hear . . .

And the inspector saw him dancing as if he were in the room with the others. The *danse macabre* looked like a scene in a black-and-white film, in the quivering light filtering through the shutters . . .

At that moment, what Montalbano was fearing would happen, happened.

As he was imagining the scene in his head, little by little Manzella's naked, bloodied body began to transform itself, becoming slowly more hairy, and the floor was no longer tiled but made of sand, exactly like the beach at Marinella . . .

In a sort of burst of light, a blinding flash, he found himself as on that morning, watching the seagull perform its dance of death.

The bird, however, was not emitting the heartrending cry he'd heard that day. It now had a human voice, that of Manzella begging for mercy and weeping . . .

And he heard, quite clearly, the laughter of the other two having a good time, as they had done before . . .

The seagull was now at the point of death.

Manzella had fallen to the floor, unable to remain standing any longer, writhing as he tried to raise his head.

The seagull was waving its beak back and forth, as if wanting to put something in a spot too high to reach.

The two men then went up to Manzella, lifted him off the ground, and started dragging him about the room, working him over with the knife as the blood spattered all over the walls and furniture . . .

But before doing this, they'd granted themselves another amusement . . .

Suddenly it all ended, perhaps because a gust of wind opened the windows again.

He found himself sitting on the stairs, eyes shut tight, face in his hands.

It was over. This was what he had so feared from the first moment he'd entered that room: that one reality would ineluctably superimpose itself on another. It wasn't like a dream that comes back to you when you're awake. No, it wasn't something he'd already seen before, it was something entirely different, an aberration of reason, a momentary swerve, a short-circuit that flung you into a world utterly foreign to you, as time scrambled the past, mixing events that happened on different days together into a single present . . .

Now he felt much calmer.

He opened his eyes and looked at the spot the seagull had pointed to with its beak.

There was a picture hanging on the wall, but he couldn't quite tell what it depicted. It was too far away.

He stood up and went up to it. Four red roses. Painted as though photographed, horrendous. The kind one used to see on chocolate boxes.

His right arm moved as if by itself, independent of his will. The hand took the picture off the wall and turned the frame round. There was nothing on the back, just the brown paper covering the reverse of the canvas. His hand spread its fingers, the painting fell to the floor, the glass shattered, the bottom part of the frame came off, and a white envelope popped out halfway. The inspector was not surprised. It seemed perfectly natural, like something he'd known all along. He bent down, picked it up, and put it in his pocket.

Now there was only one thing left for him to do: get the hell out of that house as fast as possible. He headed for the door and then stopped dead in his tracks.

Fingerprints!

He must have left hundreds in every room he entered!

Then immediately he almost started laughing. He didn't give a flying fuck whether the fingerprints were found. They weren't registered anywhere, whereas those of Carmona and Sorrentino were.

Before leaving the room, he couldn't resist and went back and looked at the two used condoms on the floor near the table.

*

As soon as he got into the car, he happened to glance at his watch. And for a moment he thought it had broken.

Could it possibly be four o'clock? Was it possible he'd spent nearly three hours in that house without having the slightest sense of it?

The position of the sun, which was ducking in and out of the clouds, confirmed that the watch was running fine.

What was the explanation?

'*What is this? What the hell is he thinking? So now he's trying to convince himself that another weird thing happened inside Manzella's house?*' Montalbano Two suddenly and rather angrily asked.

'*What other thing?*' Montalbano One immediately reacted, as if stung by a wasp.

'*This business about time. Absolutely nothing paranormal happened, nothing magical, nothing mysterious, no presences, time did not stop or stand still or similar rubbish. He simply stayed in there for three hours* without noticing the time passing. So let's drop this stuff about weird and uncanny events, because nothing unusual whatsoever happened inside that house.'

'Oh, no? Then how do you explain—'

'You want an explanation? Plain and brutal? He was already upset when he entered the house, his heart was pounding because he can't tolerate violence any more, or at least the image of violence he has in his own mind. Men become rather more sensitive to certain things when going through andropause.'

'You could have spared us the mention of andropause.'

'No, I can't not talk about it, because it's the reason for everything! Look, he practically saw what happened in there. Simple as that. It's not the first time that's happened to him. And he grafted the death of the seagull onto what he saw. Which spooked him just as much. That's all. The only thing different is the way he reacted. Like an old man, with his emotions on his sleeve and tears always ready to spill. Which is not a good sign.'

'Everything you say is so damned trite! And how do you explain the fact that he found the envelope immediately?'

'Why, I suppose you think the seagull's beak pointed to where the envelope was hidden? Come on! Give me a break! It was his policing instincts that led him there! If Catarella had searched the room, he might have taken a little longer, but he would have found it in the end, too!'

Would you two please stop bothering me? the inspector interrupted. I have to drive, for Christ's sake! You practically made me run over that little kid there!

But he felt that in the end, the discussion had done

him good, put things into perspective. Since he didn't feel the least bit hungry, he stopped at the first bar he came upon and downed a double espresso.

*

'Have Augello and the others left?'

'Yessir, Chief. Already a 'alf 'our ago already. An' Signura Fazio brought the gun.'

'Go and put it in my car.'

He went into his office, took the envelope out of his pocket, and without even looking at it, slipped it into a drawer, which he locked.

He didn't want to be distracted by any new information. The most important thing for now was for Fazio to get to Palermo safe and sound.

*

The first call came in around five thirty, from Mimì.

'Totò Monzillo sends greetings,' he said.

Monzillo was a colleague from Montelusa Central, a good policeman.

'What does that mean?'

'What's it supposed to mean, Salvo? It means Monzillo's here with me in Fiacca. We ran into each other in the car park. He's got four men with him.'

'And what's he doing there?'

'He's waiting for the ambulance with Fazio, so he can

escort them to Palermo. Direct orders from Bonetti-Alderighi. So I think that means we can—'

'Return to Vigàta? Forget it!'

'But what's the use of us going along with them? To form a procession?'

'Yes.'

'Don't you think that's a little ridiculous?'

'Not in the least. You know about the metallic-blue car, you know about Carmona, and you know why they want to kill Fazio, whereas Monzillo doesn't know a damn thing.'

'You're right,' said Augello.

The inspector had been counting on that very thing: that the commissioner, as was logical, would send an escort. That way, Carmona and his pal would realize almost at once that there were two police cars accompanying the ambulance and would almost certainly drop their plans. They were killers, not kamikazes, and were fond of their stinking lives. Montalbano felt a little less worried. And so he started signing papers.

*

'We're heading off now. It's exactly six o'clock,' said Mimì.

'Thanks. Have a good trip.'

*

'We're halfway there, and everything's going smoothly. Except that it's raining a little.'

*

The fifth call, however, was late in coming. After twenty-five minutes of waiting, Montalbano started squirming nervously in his chair, and at one point his signature came out as an impenetrable scrawl. He got up, went over to the window, lit a cigarette, and at that moment Mimì rang.

'What's the holdup?'

'Listen, something crazy happened, a false alarm.'

'Are you sure it was false?'

'Absolutely. A car with two men inside passed the ambulance and then swerved and blocked the lane. It was the wet road surface. But we immediately thought it was an ambush and surrounded the vehicle. Can you imagine? The poor bastards saw eight guns pointed at them, some of them sub-machine guns. They were forced out of the car with their hands up and searched, and then the older of the two, who's got heart trouble, had a mild attack.'

'Who were they?'

'The Bishop of Patti and his secretary.'

'Fuck!'

'I don't think that's the last we're going to hear of this.'

SEVENTEEN

Augello's eighth and last call came in just before eight o'clock.

'The ambulance has just entered the infirmary. Nothing else happened. Smooth ride, except for the mix-up with the bishop. I don't think we were even followed. Listen, since we won't be back in Vigàta till about ten, I'm just going to go home, and we can talk tomorrow.'

'All right.'

*

Now at last he could look at what Manzella had written.

He opened the drawer and took out the envelope, which wasn't sealed. Inside were two sheets of paper covered with dense handwriting on both sides. He started reading.

Inspector Montalbano . . .

He gave a start in his chair, as if someone had unexpectedly called his name.

Why had Manzella addressed the letter directly to him? He continued reading.

When he had finished, he got up and started pacing slowly around the desk. After about ten laps, he took out his handkerchief and mopped his brow. He was all sweaty. What he had just read was not a letter, but a soap-covered rope to hang oneself, a loaded and cocked pistol, a lighted fuse.

*

'Hello, Mimì? Montalbano here. Sorry to bother you, but when you get to Vigàta, I want you to come straight to the office. I'll be waiting for you.'

'But I've already told Beba to make—'

'I don't give a fuck.'

'Thanks for being so understanding.'

*

'Hello, Angela? Montalbano here. Listen, I'm very sorry, but I won't be able to see you tonight.'

'Why not?'

'Something's come up. I have to stay here at the station all night. There's a huge operation involving the whole province.'

'So when can we see each other?'

'I'll ring you tomorrow afternoon around four and we can decide then. Goodbye.'

*

Going to eat was out of the question. This whole damned story was looking as if it would end up the way it had started, that is, by taking away his appetite both morning and night.

He headed for the port. There wasn't a soul on the eastern quay, whereas in the distance, on the western one, where the trawlers docked and the big refrigerated warehouses were, the powerful floodlights were already on, lighting up the evening's catch being unloaded and reloaded across the whole area.

It was by their light that Manzella had been able to see through his telescope – the concierge had been able to see through that same telescope – and it had cost them their lives.

The glow of the floodlights whitened the western sky. It looked as if they were shooting a film.

If only it were a film! the inspector thought.

But it was a true story. The intermittent beam of the lighthouse at the end of the jetty allowed him to reach the flat rock without breaking his neck or falling into the sea. He sat down, cigarette already lit.

He had to make a decision, any decision whatsoever, before Mimì arrived. Because when he talked to him, he would need strong arguments to bring him over to his side. But there were only two possible decisions to make: either jump neck-deep into this affair and risk coming away defeated and subject to disciplinary action, controversy, and rebukes, or extract themselves and sit back and watch how the others wriggled out of it. *Tertium non datur.*

For example, he could say to himself: 'You're fifty-seven years old, in the twilight of your career: why would you want to get entangled in an affair that could bring you to a bad end?'

Or he could say: 'You're fifty-seven years old, in the twilight of your career, and therefore have nothing to lose. Give it all you've got.'

'No, no, no,' said Montalbano Two. *'He was right the first time. He's no longer the right age to play the hero and start tilting at windmills.'*

'What windmills? These are real monsters!' Montalbano One revolted.

'Of course they're real monsters, and fierce, too. And that's exactly why he should step aside. He's no longer strong enough to fight them. It's not cowardice or anything like that. He must simply realize that he's no longer able to pull it off.'

'But the letter was addressed to him! Manzella was asking him personally to intervene! He can't back out!'

'Can we think rationally about this? Manzella didn't even know Montalbano. He wrote to him because he thought he would be the person assigned the investigation. It's not a personal request, can't you get that through your head?'

'Then what, in your opinion, should he do?'

'He should go to the commissioner, tell him the whole story, and give him the letter.'

'And what, again in your opinion, will the commissioner do?'

'*Almost certainly pass it on to the Secret Service.*'

'*Which would be the same as tossing it into the wastepaper basket. And flushing three dead bodies and an attempted murder down the drain.*'

In short, a fox in the henhouse and a wolf outside. And speaking of animals, what was that story about sheep he'd read in *Don Quixote*?

Ah, yes. Sancho starts telling Don Quixote the story of a shepherd who has to get his three hundred sheep across a river. He ferries them over one at a time in a little boat, begging Sancho to keep track of the crossings and warning him that if he makes a mistake, the story will end. And indeed Sancho slips up and is no longer able to keep telling Don Quixote the story to the end. Little surprise that Montalbano couldn't tell Camilleri how the story would end!

*

However, after another fifteen minutes of thinking and rethinking, mulling and remulling, he reached a decision. By his calculations, Augello wouldn't be back for another forty minutes or so. So he had a little time. It took him ten minutes to get to the western quay. The activity hadn't yet reached its peak, and there were only four trawlers unloading their catch. The bulk of the night's catch would be arriving much later. Rizzica was standing in front of warehouse number three, talking to somebody. But as soon as he recognized the inspector, he came towards him.

'You lookin' for me?'

'No. And we'll be seeing each other tomorrow, if I'm not mistaken. I believe Inspector Augello asked you to come in.'

'Yes, sir, but since you're here, I'd like to talk.'

'So let's talk.'

Rizzica headed for that place of piss and turds whose stench had already once made Montalbano nearly faint.

'No, not there,' said the inspector. 'Let's go out to the end of the quay.'

'All right,' the other consented.

'What do you have to tell me?'

'Inspector, I want to tell you straightaway just to get it off my chest. I was wrong.'

'About what?'

'When I came to you an' reported my suspicions. I was wrong.'

'So it wasn't true the captain and crew of that fishing boat were involved in drug trafficking?'

'No, sir.'

'Then why are they sometimes late coming back to port?'

'Inspector, that boat is jinxed. There's a lot o' boats, not just trawlers, even ships, that are born under a bad star. An' they carry the hex with 'em wherever they go. I had the engine changed, an' now iss never late any more. So . . .'

'You'll have to come into the station anyway, I'm

sorry. We'll set down in writing what you have to say, file a report, and then you can leave.'

They'd reached the last warehouse, almost at the end of the quay. There the floodlights weren't on, and there was no one about.

'Who does this warehouse belong to?'

'Me.'

'Why's it closed?'

'Inspector, I only use this warehouse when there's a really big catch an' the other warehouses aren't enough. Tonight I's already told that the catch isn't so big.'

Therefore that was the warehouse they took Fazio to, right after shooting him.

*

Inspector Montalbano, since you'll probably be assigned the investigation if they kill me, and they probably will, I hope that, if you are as good as people say, you'll be able to find this letter easily. This all started when, at an unusual sort of gathering in Montelusa, I met Giovanna Lonero, a thirty-year-old transsexual. Since I felt immediately attracted to her, she confided to me that she lived in almost total isolation in an apartment in Vigàta, at the disposal of her lover, whose name she refused to tell me. She only went out at night, and when her lover was away on business. I was able to get her mobile-phone number, but she didn't want mine because if her man ever found it, she could get in a lot of trouble. After that night, I called her almost every day, but her phone was either always turned off or she just wouldn't answer. Finally she answered once and said she really wanted to see me, she had been thinking about me a lot, but didn't dare let herself be seen out and about with me or any other man at all. She agreed to come to my place the next day around midnight. And so we discovered we lived very close to each other (at the time I lived in Via della Forcella, and she in Via delle Magnolie), and therefore she wouldn't need to take her car, which might have attracted attention. She arrived on time and stayed with me until five o'clock in the morning. This first encounter was followed by many more. At this point I must confess that I own a large telescope that I use to spy on people in the intimacy of their homes. One night, totally by chance, I pointed it towards the outer part of the western quay at the port, during the busy period when they unload the fishing trawlers and load the catch onto refrigerated trucks and into the refrigerated warehouses. After that time, every so often I would look away from the lit-up windows of the nearby apartment houses and watch the traffic on the quay. And that was how I happened to witness a scene that looked very strange to me. There was a refrigerated truck stationed in a much less busy spot, in front of the last warehouse at the end of the quay, and I saw four large crates being unloaded very hurriedly from this truck and then reloaded onto a trawler that immediately went off to moor inside the harbour. Meanwhile the refrigerated truck had been loaded with crates of fish and then left. Three nights later, as I was watching the same scene unfold, Giovanna arrived. She also wanted to have a look, but then immediately stepped back in horror and said: 'Oh my God, that's Franco!' The tall, slender man of about forty was her lover,

Franco Sinagra. She was upset, as if the man could see her in turn in my room. She didn't want to stay, and left not long after. Several times when we got together after that, I tried very hard to find out a little more from her. Meanwhile I got down to work on my own, and someone from my social circle (it's a very gossipy circle) told me that Franco Sinagra was the surviving representative of the Mafia family of the same name and was forced to keep his relationship with Giovanna extremely secret because strict conformity with so-called normal behaviour was still the rule among Mafiosi. On top of this he was married to the daughter of a boss from Rivera, and his father-in-law would have never forgiven him. In short, if the whole affair ever became known, he risked losing everything, all his power and wealth. Giovanna also told me he was a stingy man who had a sort of tic; that is, he needed to appropriate everything that came within his reach, to own it himself. He had even taken away two little pieces of cheap jewellery of Giovanna's, after which she nicknamed him 'the Thieving Magpie'. Anyway, little by little, I came on my own to the logical conclusion that whatever the sort of traffic he was involved in, it had to be something extremely important, if a Mafia chief was directing operations instead of some lackey. Inspector, at this point I have no qualms about admitting to you that Giovanna and I realized we were in love. If the word 'love' bothers you in this context, then replace it with the word 'passion'. And that was how I hatched a plan, without ever telling her, to eliminate Franco Sinagra so I could have Giovanna all to myself. I also managed, from hints and suggestions from her, to work out what the mysterious traffic involved: they were ferrying chemical *weapons provided by the Russian mafia to an Arab country. Involved in the traffic were two trawlers owned by a certain Rizzica, who knows everything. But there's more: Giovanna let slip that the person pulling the strings in the whole affair was the Honourable Alvaro Di Santo, currently Undersecretary of Foreign Commerce. One night she told me that Franco was supposed to be flying to Rome the following day. She was pleased with the prospect of being completely free to spend a few nights with me. I immediately disappointed her. I told her that the following day I also had to go away, to Palermo to see my mother, who was unwell. Without arousing her suspicions, I got her to tell me at what time Franco's flight was supposed to be leaving Palermo. I was so taken up by my plan, Inspector, that I didn't realize the possible consequences of my actions. To cut a long story short, I took the same flight and, in Rome, didn't once let him out of my sight. And I had a stroke of luck: I managed to take a picture of him with my phone, in a restaurant on the outskirts of town, together with Honourable Di Santo, whom I was able to identify from a photo in a copy of the parliamentary directory I had got my hands on. Then, using a camera with a telephoto lens that I'd borrowed, I photographed Franco in action with his crates. But one unlucky day a friend of mine revealed to me that while we were away (while Franco and I were away, that is), Giovanna had gone out to enjoy herself in Fiacca. In a fit of jealous rage, I decided to call Fazio and informed on everybody, including Giovanna, and broke off all relations with her. I even changed my address. But with Fazio I sort of had to beat around the bush, because Giovanna then suddenly reappeared in my life. But I found her somehow different from before. I thought: is she sincere or is she hiding something from me? Maybe she will have to answer this question herself, Inspector, when I can no longer hear her.*

Filippo Manzella

P.S.: the photos are in a safety deposit box in my name at the Vigàta branch of the Banca dell'Isola.

Mimì finished reading the letter, laid it down on the desk, and then pushed it with his index finger towards the inspector. While reading, he hadn't had the slightest reaction, and even now he was cool as a cucumber.

'First of all,' he began, 'I'd like to know how you came into possession of this letter.'

Mimì was speaking Italian, a bad sign. Maybe he wasn't as calm as he appeared. Montalbano realized he'd made a mistake in giving him the letter without a word of explanation. He improvised a modified version of what he had planned to tell him. It seemed more logical.

'I got a call from Fazio when I was in a restaurant. He'd just remembered an address that Manzella had given him. I finished eating and went there. And that's where I found the letter, which was—'

'Stop glossing over the details. I'm a cop just like you. Got that? Was the door unlocked?'

'No.'

'So how'd you get in?'

'Well, I had a key that happened—'

'When are you going to stop feeding me shit?' Augello interrupted him.

The inspector decided it was best to tell him everything.

'Were you armed?'

'No.'

'You know, with all the respect due to a superior, I must say you're a perfect idiot. Sinagra could have left someone there to guard the place.'

'Fine, but the fact is, he didn't. Can we talk reasonably?'

'About what? The letter? There's nothing to talk about. Now you're going to put it back in the envelope, give me the key that you happened to have, and so on and so forth, and I'm going to go back and put it back in the picture frame.'

'And then what?'

'And then you are going to officially order me to go and investigate what happened in that house, and I will discover that Manzella was murdered there. I'll call Forensics and arrange things so that Arquà, or someone in his place, finds the letter. Never in a million years will he turn it over to me, and despite my insistence he'll take it directly to the commissioner, at which point we can walk away whistling. As expected.'

'*Pilatus docet*, in short,' Montalbano said bitterly.

'It really gets on my nerves when you speak Latin.'

'And what do you think the commissioner will do?'

'I couldn't fucking care less.'

'I don't like your line of reasoning, Mimì.'

'Oh, no? You're the one who taught me to look at things concretely!'

'Why, aren't the things stated in the letter concrete?'

'Of course they're concrete! But totally useless. There isn't a single bit of evidence that would hold up.'

'What are you talking about? Tomorrow Rizzica's coming, and we're going to put the screws on him. He's neck-deep in this. The warehouse where the truck stops is his, the trawlers are his, and—'

'How do you know the warehouse is his?'

'He told me himself. I ran into him a few hours ago at the port, and he even told me that when he comes in today, he's going to explain how it was all a misunderstanding and that the real problem was with the trawler's engine.'

'You see? When he found out they'd shot one of us, he shat himself and came up with an alibi. And he'll have no trouble defending himself. He'll start screaming: "But I was the first person to report that something seemed fishy! Why else would I notify the police?" And bear in mind that he's more afraid of Sinagra than we are.'

'We can try another approach. We can organize a stakeout, and the minute the refrigerated trucks arrive with Sinagra, we burst in and—'

'And get the case taken away from us immediately. Can

you imagine them leaving an investigation into chemical-weapons traffic with an Arab country in the hands of a small-time police inspector and his even smaller-time assistant? No way. The spooks'll come in, the good ones and the bad ones, and two days later—'

'Undersecretary Di Santo'll come on TV and say it was all a big mistake and the substances were actually medicines for the children of Darfur.'

'I see you're starting to catch on.'

'Yes, but the photographs—'

'Salvo, assuming you even get permission to open that deposit box, assuming the photos are even there, and assuming the judge lets you keep them for more than two seconds, those photos don't mean a fucking thing!'

'What are you saying? An undersecretary eating at the same table with a Mafioso of the calibre of Franco Sinagra?'

'Oh, right! What a scandal! How shameful! No matter what they do, our elected representatives don't give a fuck any more about public opinion! They take drugs, go to whores, rob, steal, cheat, sell themselves, commit perjury, make deals with the Mafia, and what happens to them? The newspapers talk about it for, oh, three days maybe? Then everybody forgets about it. But you – you who exposed the scandal, they won't forget about you, you can count on that, and they'll make you pay for it.'

'We could ask Tommaseo for authorization to listen to Sinagra's phone conversations with—'

'With the Honourable Di Santo? But what fucking world do you live in, anyway? Nowadays there isn't a single judge who'll grant you that authorization, and he couldn't do it even if he wanted to, because these people know how to shield themselves. He would have to ask for the authorization of parliament first, and then hope and pray they granted it!'

Montalbano listened to all this with a sort of mounting fatigue. Because these were words he himself might have said. But he realized that to continue to talk to Mimì would be a waste of breath. He would never manage to make him change his position. The best thing was to send him home to bed. He sat there for a few moments in silence, as if reflecting on what Mimì had said, then leaned forward, took the envelope, put the letter back inside, and handed it to Mimì, who put it in his pocket.

'Tomorrow morning, no later than eight, I want you to go to Via Bixio. Take Gallo, and leave Galluzzo with me here.'

'All right. But sleep easy. It couldn't have been done any other way.'

*

In the light of ignoble common sense, no, it couldn't have been done any other way. The argument Mimì had just made was his own, yes, but it was only the first part of the argument that he, in Mimì's place, would have made.

The second part, in fact, would have begun as follows:

granted all of the above, what can we do now to screw them all, from the Honourable Di Santo to Franco Sinagra, without having to take it up the you-know-what ourselves? That was the question.

He would have to find the answer all by himself. By coming up with an idea that it scared him even to think about. Dropping everything was not an option.

EIGHTEEN

As he got up to go home, his mobile phone rang. It was Angela.

'Listen, are you still at the station?' she asked.

'Yes, why?'

'I want to see you, even if it's only for five minutes. I have something extremely important to tell you.'

She was scared, and her voice sounded choked. But he didn't want to waste any time with her. He absolutely needed to go home to Marinella and reflect in peace.

'I already told you it's not possible. Has something happened?'

'I've heard from that person I told you about.'

Carmona. Like all fugitives from justice, he came and went as he pleased without anyone, police and carabinieri included, ever recognizing him.

'What did he want?'

'To know if we were seeing each other tonight. I told

261

him you were busy and we would see each other tomorrow. And then he told me I had to do something.'

'What was that?'

'I can't tell you over the phone.'

She was very scared. Her voice was trembling.

'Try to stay calm. You can tell me tomorrow evening.'

'No. I absolutely have to tell you tonight, so that you can—'

'All right, listen, I can see you for five minutes, but let's meet halfway between here and Fiacca, so I can get back to the station as quickly as possible. Have you finished your shift?'

'I got off fifteen minutes ago.'

'Do you know the Torrisi Motel? If we leave right now, we can meet there in forty-five minutes. Oh, and don't get out of your car when you arrive, just wait for me in the car park. And make sure nobody follows you.'

*

While driving there, he was thinking not of what he would say to Angela, but of how to corner Sinagra and, by association, Di Santo with him. Because what Mimì had called to his attention was all well and good, but it was also true that everything has its limits. For example: it's one thing to go out to eat with someone vaguely associated with the Mafia, and it's another thing to be seen in the company of a Mafioso publicly known to have ordered two murders and another attempted murder.

Knowledge of the fact would make Sinagra's arrest all the more sensational and the public disgracing of the honourable undersecretary all the more effective. So the problem came down to one thing only: how to screw Sinagra?

When the inspector pulled into the car park, which was almost entirely in darkness, he still hadn't found an answer.

He got out of the car. There were three other cars in the lot. One flashed its lights.

'Get in,' said Angela, opening the car door.

The moment he was inside, she threw her arms around him and gave him a long kiss.

'I'm not sure I wasn't followed,' she said in a low voice as the inspector, still numb from the unexpected attack, was regaining consciousness. 'So we should pretend we're meeting here to . . .'

'Then let's get into the back seat,' Montalbano suggested. 'Like lovers who, even when they have only five minutes . . .'

They got out and got into the back.

'Lie down,' Angela ordered him.

The inspector obeyed and, after climbing on top of him, with her left leg on the seat next to his and her right foot resting on the floor of the car, she held him tight. Montalbano couldn't move.

'Carmona told me that tomorrow night I'm supposed to make you drink a lot and get very tired. And that when I see that you are in a deep sleep . . .'

The problem was that when she spoke in her present state of agitation, moving her hips one minute and her breasts the next, it had a devastating effect on the inspector.

'. . . when I see that you are in a deep sleep, I am supposed to go and open the door to let them in. But are you listening to me?'

'Hmm?' said Montalbano.

At that exact moment he was reviewing in his mind Book I of *The Iliad*, 'Sing, goddess, the anger of Peleus' son Achilleus . . .',* after having first tried to think in rapid succession of the last funeral he'd been to, two or three massacres, and an old woman who'd been murdered and cut up . . . But the girl's weight, body heat, and breath were too much for him to blot out. He was making a superhuman effort to make what he was feeling, well, intangible.

'They want me to open—'

'Right, right, I got that. But why?'

'Carmona says they want to photograph you naked with me beside you, also naked. To blackmail you.'

'And why was it so urgent for you to tell me this?'

'Because I'm not convinced that all they want to do is take your picture. And also to let you know, so that you can maybe catch Carmona in the act.'

'You're right. I'll see what I can do, thanks.'

---

* Richmond Lattimore's translation.

Detached, yes, but always polite, our Inspector Montalbano. Always *compos sui* (but why the hell was he thinking in Latin?), even when he had a beautiful young woman lying on top of him.

'And now, I'm sorry,' he said, 'but I really have to go.'

Angela got off him, he sat up, and they got out of the car and kissed. Exactly like two lovers who had just released a little of their pent-up desire.

'I'll ring you tomorrow,' the inspector said.

He waited for her to leave, then went into the motel.

'Excuse me, but could I use your bathroom?' he asked the porter, who knew him.

'Of course, Inspector.'

Locking himself inside, he took off his jacket and shirt, turned on the tap, and put his steaming head under the running water.

*

Compromising photos, right! They would take those afterwards, since the way things would have gone would have been as follows: Carmona and his friend would have gone into his house with the camera and had Angela lie down next to him, naked. Then Carmona would have pulled out his gun and killed them both. Almost a repeat of what they did to Manzella. Then they would have arranged the corpses in more or less obscene poses and photographed them. The newspaper and TV headlines: **Inspector Montalbano And His Young Lover Killed**

While Sleeping. A Crime Of Passion? And then it would turn out that they were shot by some jealous ex-lover of Angela. Everybody'd already seen the movie, but people never tired of seeing it again.

But why were they aiming at him? Maybe Mimì was right. Maybe the Via Bixio house *was* under surveillance. Their suspicions must have been aroused when the inspector didn't immediately call Forensics but kept the whole business to himself. This silence got them worried and upset. They must have thought: if Montalbano is acting this way, it must mean he found something very damning to us in there. Better silence him before he takes any action.

And this meant he didn't have much time left to neutralize Sinagra. Now it was an open duel.

*

He needed to remain lucid for at least another two hours. He prepared the large espresso pot, and when the coffee bubbled up, he took the whole thing out to the veranda. The night was a little chilly, and he also felt chilled for his own reasons, as the weariness of the day began to make itself felt. But he didn't put his jacket back on to go outside. The cold actually helped him to think. By now he knew Manzella's letter by heart and could repeat it to himself word for word. Which was what he started to do, changing registers each time: first as a lament, then stressing practically every syllable, then pausing after each line.

The fifth time through, one sentence in particular struck him: *a stingy man who had a sort of tic; he would appropriate everything that came within his reach . . . Giovanna had nicknamed him 'the Thieving Magpie'.*

The Thieving Magpie. What did it mean? Why did this seem so important to him? The phrase started repeating itself in his head, together with certain passages of Rossini's music, the way it used to happen with old vinyl records when the needle would get stuck on a single syllable or note.

At last there was a flash of light.

A crazy thought, real loony-bin stuff, like betting everything he owned on the roulette wheel — no, better yet, like a sort of Russian roulette, a game of chance where if he got it wrong, he would be out of the police force the very next day. But he couldn't think of anything else, and it seemed like the best option.

He studied it from every possible, imaginable angle. With a little luck, it might work. He looked at his watch. Two a.m.

He got up, went into the house, and dialled Angela's number. After calming her down from the fright he'd given her, he asked her: 'Do you have some old female relative that you can think of, say, over eighty, preferably a widow, half senile, who doesn't live in Fiacca but is in the phone book?'

'Have you gone crazy?'

'Almost. Do you or don't you?'

'Well, there's Aunt 'Ntunietta . . .'

'Excellent. Now listen to me very carefully.'

He then took a shower and went to bed. He slept soundly and peacefully, like a baby, until seven.

*

The telephone rang at seven thirty, as planned. He'd barely had time to have a quick shower, shave, and drink a cup of coffee.

'Hello?'

'MontalbanothisisTommaseowhat'sthisbusinessabouta letterfromayoungwomanyouhaven'tanswered?'

The prosecutor spoke as if all the words were stuck together. He sounded quite agitated.

'What letter, sir?' Montalbano asked, feigning great surprise.

'A young woman with a very sensuous voice, among other things?'

Tommaseo stopped. He must have heard Angela's voice again in his mind. Whenever a case had anything to do with women, the prosecutor lost his head.

'I'm sorry, but I have to go and get a drink of water.'

He returned a few moments later, speaking normally.

'. . . Her name is Antonietta Vullo, from Rivera, she says she sent you a letter in which she claims that a certain Franco Sinagra is holding a transsexual named Giovanna Lonero prisoner at his residence in Via Roma 28 and routinely and repeatedly torturing this man – I mean, er, woman. But you've done nothing about this letter. Why not?'

'To be honest, the whole story seemed a little far-fetched to me.'

'Look, I can tell you that Antonietta Vullo is in the Rivera phone book. She's real. Did you call her up to check? No, right? Well, I did!'

Montalbano turned frosty. 'And what did she tell you?'

'An old woman answered the phone, she sounded senile. I couldn't understand a word she said. She must be the girl's grandmother. But she said she wasn't there. At any rate, I've already sent you a search warrant, Montalbano.'

'Look, sir, this is a complicated matter. This Franco Sinagra is a Mafia boss with some very powerful friends.'

'You know what the girl said to me, Montalbano? That if we don't immediately try to free this man – I mean, this transsexual – she will go straight to the newspapers and television. So, if the story turns out to be true, we'll all be neck-deep in shit. Because we didn't take a letter seriously even though it was signed by a real person with a real address. Speaking of which, do you still have it?'

'Nah, I threw it away.'

'It doesn't matter. But it would be a serious breach of duty not to clear this up. Do you understand?'

'And what, sir, if the whole thing turns out to be the fantasy of a crazy girl? How will Sinagra react?'

'If you don't find the wom— I mean, the transsexual, you'll find something else, I'm sure of it. Can you imagine not finding anything in a Mafioso's—'

'All right, sir, if you put it that way . . . I guess I have no choice but to follow your orders.'

'As well you should, for once.'

*

'Zito? Montalbano here.'

'What's up?'

'I want to return the favour you did for Fazio. I want you and a cameraman here in Vigàta at Via Roma 28, in half an hour. But don't let yourselves be seen before I arrive.'

'But Via Roma 28 is Franco Sinagra's house!'

'Exactly.'

'Fuck!'

As soon as he hung up, the inspector rang the station and asked for Galluzzo. Once he'd given him instructions, he called Mimì.

'Are you at Via Bixio?'

'Yeah, it looks like a massacre took place in there. I called Forensics immediately and am now outside waiting for them. I couldn't stay inside.'

'Don't tell me you felt metaphysically disconcerted!'

'Metaphysically, no. But did you see the condoms on the floor? Do you realize what they did to Manzella? Who are these animals, anyway? Oh, and listen, I almost forgot to tell you: Arquà's coming in person, know what I mean? What are you going to do?'

'I'm on my way to headquarters; Tommaseo's looking for me.'

'Oh, yeah? What's he want?'

'Dunno.'

*

The two squad cars arrived about twenty minutes later. Galluzzo, who was driving the first one, handed the inspector the warrant and let him in on the passenger's side. The other car was driven by Lamarca, who was accompanied by another young officer, Di Grado.

'Do exactly as I do,' Galluzzo said to Lamarca.

As they entered Vigàta, Galluzzo put on the siren and started racing as if chasing a speeding car. Lamarca did the same. Pedestrians jumped onto the pavements, hurling curses and epithets at them as they passed. Total pandemonium, in short. Galluzzo came to a screeching halt in front of the house at Via Roma 28, then got out of the car with a sub-machine gun in his hand while the inspector jumped out of the other side. Out of the corner of his eye, he saw the door of a car parked nearby fly open, and Zito and his cameraman came out. A window on the top floor of the house opened partway and was immediately closed.

Before ringing the doorbell, Montalbano gave Lamarca and Di Grado, also holding sub-machine guns, the time to take up positions well in view of the TV camera. Meanwhile, a great number of rubberneckers started gathering round.

Come one, come all, ladies and gentlemen, to the great fireworks spectacular of the award-winning Salvo Montalbano & Co.! Who knows what you'll see? Maybe the master pyrotechnician himself will get roasted to death in one of his own fireballs, but whatever happens, you can be sure to see a show you'll never forget! Come one, come all!

So, when ringing the doorbell, he heard its chimes as a cross between a Gloria and a Requiem.

'Who's there?' asked a frightened female voice.

'Police! Open up!'

The door opened, and a woman of about thirty-five with black hair and big eyes appeared, a hot-blooded sort, but scared out of her wits.

'Are you Mrs Sinagra?'

'Yes, but ... my husband's not here.'

'It doesn't matter. We have a search warrant. Please let us in and then close the door immediately.'

She stood aside. The ground floor consisted of a large living room, a dining room, bathroom, and kitchen. They found nothing there.

Montalbano went upstairs, and the first thing he saw, inside a sort of study, was Manzella's telescope in front of the window. On the desk was the case for the binoculars. For an instant, his knees buckled, and he grabbed Galluzzo to keep from falling.

'You feel OK, Chief?'

'I feel fantastic, Gallù!'

The triumphal march from Verdi's *Aida* had started playing in his head. As he'd imagined, the thieving magpie hadn't been able to resist the allure of the sparkling chrome telescope! And he'd dug his own grave.

In a small bedroom, they found a single bed unmade and still warm. But it was clear that two people had slept in the double bed in the master bedroom.

The inspector went back downstairs, sat in an armchair, and lit a cigarette. Mrs Sinagra, sitting in front of him, had gone from pale to increasingly red in the face. She was starting to get angry, and with every noise the policemen made upstairs, she became more upset.

In the end she blurted out: 'Mind telling me what you're looking for?'

In his mind, Montalbano flipped a proverbial coin. He'd already won, because Sinagra would have a very hard time explaining what Manzella's telescope and binoculars were doing in his house. But he wasn't satisfied yet. He wanted to have the man himself, Franco Sinagra, in his hands. The coin fell to the ground: heads. And so Montalbano decided to take another gamble.

'I have no problem answering that, signora. We're looking for a woman.'

'A woman? What woman?' Mrs Sinagra asked in shock.

'A transsexual named Giovanna Lonero, with whom your husband Franco has been in a relationship for some time, and who—'

'Ahhhhhhh!'

It was a sort of roar so loud and unexpected that Montalbano leapt to his feet. He could hear over his head the footsteps of the three men upstairs scrambling down the stairs to see what was happening.

'They tried to tell me! Ahhhhh! They tried to tell me! Ahhhhh! An' I's too stupid to listen! Ahhhhh!'

'Calm down, signora, stop that!'

'That goddamn son of a stinking whore! Jesus, how disgusting! Yechhh! Ahhhhh! With someone you don' even know if iss a man or a woman! I'm going to kill the stinkin' bastard wit' my own hands!'

They were unable to hold her back, and she dashed into the kitchen and moved an enormous fridge on wheels out of position. Montalbano immediately understood.

'Lamarca, take her into another room.'

Despite the fact that the young officer was strong and burly, he had a rather hard time dragging away the woman, who had stopped roaring and was now crying.

The inspector bent down to examine the floor carefully and noticed a few tiles that formed a sort of single block.

'This is a trapdoor. Galluzzo and Di Grado, try and see if you can open it.'

After fifteen minutes of trying, they still hadn't succeeded.

Montalbano then noticed a small button next to the plug socket of the fridge. He pressed it with one finger, and the trapdoor opened without a sound. The classic Mafia rabbit hole with no escape. As Galluzzo and Di Grado pointed their sub-machine guns, the inspector bent down towards the entrance and, cupping his hands around his mouth, said:

'Come out immediately, or I'm going to throw a hand grenade down there!'

Galluzzo and Di Grado looked at him, mystified. Hand grenade? Where? At that moment the raised hands and then the scarred face of Vittorio Carmona, killer and bodyguard, appeared.

'Cuff him! He's wanted for murder!' the inspector ordered.

Then Franco Sinagra popped out. He was in his underpants and carrying his clothes.

'You're under arrest for ordering the murders of Filippo Manzella and Matilde Verruso, and for the attempted murder of Inspector Fazio.'

'Can I get dressed?'

'No.'

*

It was a day of bedlam. News reporters, TV cameras, telephone interviews, the commissioner pissed off because that idiot Arquà had turned over to him a hot letter that he should actually have given to Montalbano, and in so doing, got him into trouble, Tommaseo completely in the dark as to everything and going around saying it was thanks to him that Sinagra was seen on all the national television news programmes in his underpants . . .

*

Around nine o'clock that evening, as the inspector was driving home to Marinella, his phone rang. It was Angela.

'Just a minute,' he said.

He pulled over to the side of the road before speaking again.

'Angela, thank you so much for everything. You were brilliant! You performed marvellously with Prosecutor Tommaseo! If not for you . . . How did you find out, anyway?'

'What do you mean, how did I find out? The TV news programmes have been talking about nothing else! Why didn't you call me?'

He'd quite simply forgotten.

'I'm sorry, Angela, but with all that was happening . . .'

'I understand.'

'Now you have nothing more to be afraid of. No one can blackmail and force you to do anything you don't want to do.'

'You know, Salvo, I was thinking . . .'

'Tell me.'

'Don't take it the wrong way. But, well, since there's no longer any reason for us to see each other . . .'

A punch in the stomach. But of course she was right. What reason was there for them to see each other?

'You won't be coming to my place tonight.'

'Don't be offended, Salvo. Try and understand me.'

'I'm not offended, I understand you perfectly.'

'I'm sorry, OK? And give me a ring whenever you like. Goodbye.'

'Goodbye.'

Sitting out on the veranda, with a touch of melancholy to keep him company, he tried to console himself with a dish – a huge one – of *caponata*.

Author's Note

Like *The Wings of the Sphinx*, this novel had its origin in a press clipping sent to me by my providential friend Maurizio Assalto, whom I thank warmly. And apparently it's not entirely superfluous to declare that all the characters, situations, episodes, and places in this story belong to my imagination and not to the real world. But when one writes, even pure fiction, isn't one's reference always the real world?

Notes

page 9 – **Zingarelli's a dictionary**: Zingarelli's is one of the standard dictionaries of modern Italian.

page 49 – **municipal police officer**: what Italians call a *vigile urbano* is part of a different department of law enforcement from the *commissariato*, of which Montalbano is chief, and which handles criminal cases.

page 105 – **'madhouse' 'But weren't they abolished?'**: in 1978, the passage of Law 180 (also known as the Franco Basaglia Law, after the famous psychiatrist-neurologist who inspired it) technically abolished insane asylums in Italy. Among other things, it eliminated 'dangerousness' as an acceptable reason for internment. It did stipulate, however, that 'obligatory mental health treatment' (*Trattamento Sanitario Obbligatorio*, or TSO) must be applied to individuals whose 'psychological disturbances are such as to require urgent therapy', if such therapy is not voluntarily accepted by the persons in question. Care to the mentally ill would be provided by a variety of institutions, including outpatient clinics, community centres, and 'residential' and 'semi-residential' centres. Law 180 was slow in being applied. The first Berlusconi government moved in 1994 to close the remaining sanatoriums still open. But, as it turns out, the current system makes available to patients far more psychiatric services than before; the 'residential centres' are, in effect, psychiatric hospitals. The inflexibly coercive nature of the pre-1978 asylums has, however, been considerably diminished.

page 124 – **Ragionier Muscetta:** Ragioniere is a largely meaningless title given to accountants whose specialization does not go beyond that provided by vocational college. A full certified accountant is called a *contabile.*

page 125 – **'like one of those carabinieri jokes':** the carabinieri are often the butt of jokes in Italy, always having to do with their lack of intelligence.

page 141 – **Monsieur Lapalisse:** a reference to the legendary Jacques de la Palisse (1470–1525), a French nobleman and military officer active in Francis I's Italian campaign, during which he was killed.

His epitaph reads: *Ci gît Monsieur de La Palice: S'il n'était pas mort, il ferait encore envie* ('Here lies Monsieur de la Palisse: Were he not dead, he would still be envied'). This was originally misread – by mistake, presumably – as saying '. . . *S'il n'était pas mort, il serait encore en vie*' ('Were he not dead, he would still be alive'), due perhaps to the potential confusion between f and s in serif script. The misreading gave rise to a whole tradition of burlesque song variants, with similar tautological plays on words, such as *Il n'eût pas eu son pareil / S'il avait été seul au monde* ('He would have had no equals / Had he been alone in the world'). The many variants were brought together into *La chanson de La Palisse* by Bernard de la

Monnoye in the early eighteenth century, though other versions exist as well.

page 211 – **'if I sing the song, i' comes out Surrientino'**: Neapolitan dialect for Sorrentino.

page 213 – **Via Piscio**: i.e., 'Piss Street'.

page 248 – ***Tertium non datur***: 'No third possibility is given' (Latin).

page 255 – **Mimì was speaking Italian, a bad sign**: i.e., instead of Sicilian.

page 256 – ***Pilatus docet***: 'As Pilate teaches', that is, it's better not to dirty one's hands (Latin).

If you enjoyed **The Dance of the Seagull,** *you'll love*

THE TREASURE HUNT

the latest Inspector Montalbano mystery

Montalbano opened the door to step out. But Gallo held him back, putting one hand on his arm.

'What's in there, Chief?'

'If it's what I think, it's something so horrific that it'll haunt your dreams for the rest of your life...'

When a crazed elderly man and his sister begin firing bullets from their balcony down onto the Vigata street below, Inspector Montalbano finds himself a reluctant television hero.

A few days later, when a letter arrives containing a mysterious riddle, the Inspector becomes drawn into a perplexing treasure hunt set by an anonymous challenger. As the hunt intensifies, Montalbano is relieved to be offered the assistance of Arturo Pennisi, a young man eager to witness the detective's investigative skills first hand.

Avoiding meddling commissioners and his irate girlfriend, Livia, the inspector will follow the treasure hunt's clues and travel from Vigata's teeming streets to its deserted outskirts: where an abandoned house overlooks a seemingly bottomless lake. But when a horrifying crime is committed, the game must surely be laid aside. And it isn't long before Montalbano himself will be in terrible danger...

Out now

An extract follows here...

ONE

That Gregorio Palmisano and his sister Caterina had been church people since childhood was known all over town. They never missed a single morning or evening service, not a single Holy Mass or vespers, and sometimes they even went to church for no reason other than the fact that they felt like it. For the Palmisanos, the faint scent of incense and candle wax lingering in the air after the Mass was better than the smell of *ragù* to a man who hadn't eaten for ten days.

Always kneeling in the first pew, they didn't bow their heads when praying, but held them high, eyes open wide. But they weren't looking at the great crucifix over the main altar or the Blessed Virgin in sorrow at its feet. No, they never once, not even for a second, took their eyes off the priest, and they watched his every move: the way he turned the pages of the Gospel, the way he gave his benediction, the way he raised his arms when he said *Dominus vobiscum* and then concluded with *Ite, missa est.*

The truth was that they would have both liked to be priests themselves, to wear surplices, stoles, and vestments, to open the little door of the tabernacle, hold the silver chalice in their hands, administer Holy Communion to the faithful. Both of them, Caterina, too.

In fact when, as a little girl, she told her mother, Matilde, what she wanted to do when she grew up, her mama firmly corrected her.

'You mean a nun,' she said.

'No, Mamma, a priest.'

'What? And why do you want to be a priest and not a nun?' Signora Matilde asked with a laugh.

'Because the priest says Mass, and the nuns don't.'

In the end they were both forced to work for their father, who was a wholesaler of foodstuffs, which he kept crammed in three large warehouses, one next to the other.

After their parents died, Gregorio and Caterina changed their merchandise, and instead of pasta, tins of tomato paste, and dried cod, they started selling antiques. It was Gregorio's job to go around to the oldest churches in the neighbouring towns and the half-dilapidated palazzi of nobles once rich and now starving. One of their three warehouses was chock-full of crucifixes, ranging from the kind you hang from your neck on a chain to the life-size variety. There were even three or four naked crosses, huge, heavy replicas of the original, designed for being carried on the shoulder of a penitent during Holy Week processions, as Roman centurions scourged him.

When he turned seventy and she was sixty-eight, they sold the three warehouses, but overnight they took a certain amount of objects to their home on the top floor of a building next to the town hall. It was a big apartment with six spacious rooms and a terrace, which the two never used, too big for a brother and sister who had never wanted to marry and had no nephews or nieces.

Their religious obsession increased with the reality of no longer having anything to do. They went out only to go to church, always side by side, walking fast, heads down, never returning greetings, only to race back home afterwards and lock themselves in, shutters always closed, as if they were eternally in mourning.

The grocery shopping was done by a woman who used to clean the warehouses for them, but they never allowed her into their apartment. In the morning she would find a small piece of paper pinned to the door, on which Caterina had written everything she needed, and the necessary money under the doormat.

When she returned, she would put the bags down on the floor, knock, and call out, before leaving: 'The groceries!'

They didn't own a television, and when they were still antiques dealers, nobody had ever seen them reading a book or a newspaper, but only the breviary, the way priests do.

After about ten years of this, something changed. The Palmisanos stopped going outside, stopped going to church, and never looked out from their balcony, not even when the procession of the town's patron saint went by.

Their only contact, oral or written, with the outside world was with the woman who did the shopping.

One morning the people of Vigàta noticed that between the first and second balconies of the Palmisanos' apartment they had hung a large white banner on which were these words, in large block letters: SINNERS, REPENT!

A week later, between the second and third balconies, another banner appeared: SINNERS, WE WILL PUNISH YOU!

The following week a third one appeared, but this time it covered the entire terrace balustrade and was the largest of all: WE WILL MAKE YOU PAY FOR YOUR SINS WITH YOUR LIFE!!!

When he saw the third banner, Montalbano was worried.

'Don't make me laugh!' Mimì Augello said to him. 'They're a couple of senile old people who happen to be religious fanatics!'

'Bah!'

'Why are you not convinced?'

'The exclamation marks. There are suddenly three, where before there was one.'

'So?'

'It may be a sign that they're giving the sinners a deadline, and this is the last warning.'

'But who would these sinners happen to be?'

'We're all sinners, Mimì. Have you forgotten? Do you know whether Gregorio Palmisano has a firearms licence?'

'I'll go and check.' He returned almost immediately, frowning slightly. 'Yes, he's got a licence all right. He requested it when he was dealing in antiques and it was granted. A revolver. But he also declared two hunting rifles and a pistol that used to belong to his father.'

'Listen, tomorrow I want you to ask Fazio what church they used to go to, and then go and talk to the parish priest.'

'But he's sworn to the secrecy of the confessional!'

'And you're not going to ask him to reveal any secrets; you only need to find out just how far gone he thinks they are, and whether he thinks their madness is dangerous or not. In the meantime I'll phone the mayor.'

'What for?'

'I want him to send a municipal policeman to the Palmisanos' place to take down those banners.'

*

Officer Landolina of the Municipal Police arrived at the Palmisanos' home at seven in the evening. Since the Palermo match was coming on TV immediately after the evening news, he wanted to take care of things early, go home, eat, and settle into his armchair.

He knocked on the door, but nobody answered. Since Landolina, a stubborn but scrupulous man, didn't want to waste any time, he not only continued knocking as hard as he could, with his clenched fist, but also started kicking the door until an elderly man called out: 'Who is it?'

'Police! Open the door!'

'No.'

'Open the door right now!'

'Go away, Officer, if you know what's good for you!'

'Don't threaten me! Open up!'

Gregorio stopped threatening him and simply fired his revolver once through the door.

The bullet grazed Landolina's head, and he turned tail and ran.

After descending the stairs and going out into the main street, he saw people fleeing in every direction amidst cries and laments, curses and prayers. From two separate balconies, Gregorio and Caterina had started firing rifles at passers-by below.

Thus began the siege of the Palmisanos' little fortress by the forces of order – that is, by Montalbano, Augello, Fazio, Gallo, and Galluzzo. The crowd of onlookers was large but kept at a distance by the municipal policemen. After an hour or so, the newspapermen and television crews also arrived.

By ten o'clock that evening, seeing that not even their priest, equipped with a megaphone, could persuade his two elderly parishioners to surrender, Montalbano came to the conclusion that they would have to storm the tiny stronghold. He sent Fazio out to determine how they could reach the terrace, either from the roof or a neighbouring apartment. After an hour of careful reconnaissance, Fazio returned to say that it was hopeless: there was no way to reach the roof from any of the other apartments or to approach the Palmisanos' terrace.

The inspector rang Catarella from his mobile. 'Call the Montelusa fire department at once—'

'Izz 'ere a fire, Chief?'

'Let me finish! And tell them to come here at once with a ladder that can reach the fifth floor.'

'So there's a fire onna fifth floor?'

'There isn't a fire!'

'So why's you want the fire department?' Catarella asked with implacable logic.

Cursing the saints, the inspector hung up, dialled the fire department himself, identified himself, and explained what he wanted.

'Right away?' the switchboard operator asked.

'Of course!'

'The problem is that the two vehicles with ladders are engaged. They could probably be in Vigàta in about an hour. As for the searchlight, there's no problem. I'll send the crew right away.'

Right away meant another hour wasted.

Every so often the Palmisanos would fire a few shots with their rifles and pistols, just to stay sharp. At last the searchlight arrived, got into position, and cast its beam. The entire facade of the building was bathed in a harsh blue light.

'Thank you, Inspector Montalbano!' the television cameramen cried out.

It looked exactly as if they were shooting a film.

The ladder eventually arrived after one o'clock in the morning, and was promptly extended until it touched the balustrade covered by the banner.

'All right, I'm going up,' said Montalbano. 'Fazio, you come up behind me. Mimì, you go inside with Gallo and Galluzzo and wait outside their door. While I'm keeping them busy on the terrace, I want you to try to force their door and get inside.'

No sooner had the inspector set his foot on the first rung than Gregorio suddenly appeared from behind the banner and fired his pistol. And disappeared. Montalbano took cover in a doorway and said to Fazio: 'I think it's better if I go up alone. You stay behind on the ground and start firing to give me some cover.'

As soon as Fazio fired his first shot, tearing a hole in the banner, the inspector climbed the first rung. He was gripping the ladder with only his left hand, since he had his revolver in his right.

He continued climbing cautiously. He'd reached the fourth floor when suddenly, despite Fazio's gunfire, Gregorio Palmisano reappeared and fired a shot from his revolver that barely missed the inspector.

Instinctively Montalbano ducked his head between his shoulders, and in so doing he caught sight of the street below. All at once a cold sweat drenched him from head to toe and he began to feel so dizzy he was in danger of falling. A surge of vomit rose from the pit of his stomach. He realized that he was in the throes of vertigo, something he'd never experienced before. And now, no doubt with the onset of old age, it suddenly appeared at the worst possible moment.

He held still for a long minute, unable to move, eyes shut tight. But then he clenched his teeth and resumed his climb, even more slowly than before.

When he reached the balustrade, he bolted upright, ready to start firing, but a quick glance revealed that the terrace was deserted. Gregorio had gone back inside, closing the French windows behind him, and must certainly be behind the shutter with his revolver pointed.

'Turn off the spotlight!' Montalbano yelled.

And he leapt onto the terrace, immediately lying flat. Gregorio's shot arrived on schedule, but the harsh light that had suddenly gone out had left him dazzled, forcing him to fire blindly. Montalbano fired back in turn, but couldn't see anything. Then little by little his eyes returned to normal.

But standing up and running towards the French windows while shooting was out of the question, since this time Gregorio was certain to hit him.

As he was wondering what to do, Fazio jumped over the balustrade and lay down beside him.

Now they heard rifle shots coming from inside.

'That's Caterina firing at our men from behind the door,' Fazio said softly.

The terrace was completely bare except for a vase of flowers and a clothesline with things hanging from it; as for anything behind which they might take cover, nothing. Leaning against a wall, however, were three or four long iron poles, possibly the remains of an old belvedere.

'What should we do?' asked Fazio.

'Run over there and grab one of those poles. If it's not rusted through, I think you should be able to burst open the French windows. Give me your gun. Ready? Here we go . . . One, two, three!'

They stood up, and Montalbano started shooting both pistols, feeling slightly ridiculous, like a sheriff in an American movie. Then he stopped up alongside Fazio, who was using the pole as a lever, still shooting, this time at the shutter. At last the French windows flew open, and they found themselves in near total darkness, because the large room they had entered was barely illuminated by the faint light of an oil lamp on a small table. It had been some time since the Palmisanos stopped using electric lights, and no doubt they no longer had power.

Where was the crazy old man hiding? They heard two rifle shots ring out in a nearby room. It was Caterina fighting off the efforts of Mimì, Gallo, and Galluzzo to break down the front door.

'Grab her from behind,' Montalbano said to Fazio, giving him back his gun. 'I'll go and look for Gregorio.'

Fazio disappeared behind a door that gave onto a corridor.

But there was another door off the room, and it was closed. Montalbano felt certain, for no particular reason, that the old man was behind it. Tiptoeing up to it, he turned the knob, and the door opened slightly. The expected gunshot never came.

And so he flung the door wide open while jumping aside. There was no reaction.

And what was Fazio up to? Why was the old lady still firing?

He took a deep breath and went in, bent completely over, ready to shoot. And immediately he didn't know where he was.

It was a large room, densely thicketed with a sort of forest, but of what?

Then he realized what it was and felt paralysed by an irrational fear.

By the light of another oil lamp he saw dozens and dozens of crucifixes of varying size, ranging from three feet to ceiling-high, held upright by wooden bases and forming indeed a tangled forest, arranged in such a way that many faced one another, with the arm of one cross cutting across the arm of the cross beside it, while other, shorter crosses had their backs to the larger crosses but stood face to face with other crosses of the same height, and so on.

Montalbano became immediately convinced that Gregorio was not in the room and certainly would never start firing and risk striking one of the crucifixes. All the same, he couldn't move, being frozen in fear like a child who finds himself alone in an empty church illuminated only by candlelight. At the far end of the large room was an open door, with the dim light of yet another oil lamp filtering through. The inspector eyed it but was unable to take a single step.